DESTINATION UNKNOWN

REMNANTS™

DESTINATION UNKNOWN

K.A. APPLEGATE

AN
APPLE
PAPERBACK

SCHOLASTIC INC.
New York Toronto London Auckland Sydney
Mexico City New Delhi Hong Kong Buenos Aires

(For Michael and Jake)

No part of this publication may be reproduced in whole or in part, or stored in a retrieval system, or transmitted in any form or by any means, electronic, mechanical, photocopying, recording, or otherwise, without written permission of the publisher. For information regarding permission, write to Scholastic Inc., Attention: Permissions Department, 555 Broadway, New York, NY 10012.

ISBN 0-590-88074-8

Copyright © 2001 by Katherine Applegate.
All rights reserved. Published by Scholastic Inc.
SCHOLASTIC, APPLE PAPERBACKS, and associated logos are trademarks and/or registered trademarks of Scholastic Inc.
REMNANTS and associated logos are trademarks and/or registered trademarks of Katherine Applegate.

12 11 10 9 8 7 6 5 4 3 2 1   1 2 3 4 5 6 7/0

Printed in the U.S.A.
First Scholastic printing, September 2001

It took less than a year for Billy Weir to lose his mind.

He lay still, absolutely still, unable to move a muscle, unable to move his eyes, unable to control his breathing, paralyzed, utterly, absolutely paralyzed.

The technology of the hibernation berth had worked. It was ninety-nine-point-nine-percent successful. It had stopped his heart, his kidneys, his liver. It had stopped every system, down to the cellular level.

It had failed to still his mind.

The system supplied his minuscule needs for oxygen and water and nutrition. But it did nothing for the sleepless consciousness imprisoned in the all-but-dead body.

He raved silently. He hallucinated. He regained his sanity and lost it and regained it as the years passed, as the decades passed, as the very definition of madness became irrelevant.

He was in hell. He was in heaven. He floated, disembodied. He was chained to his own corpse. He rose and sank. He thought and imagined, and he almost flickered out, extinguished.

He begged for death.

And all of it over again, again, again. Time was nothing, leaping by in years and decades, crawling past so slowly that each millisecond might be a century.

In his madness he remembered every memory. He remembered when his name was Ruslan, not William. He remembered the cold and loneliness of the orphanage in Chechnya after his parents were killed.

He remembered his adoptive parents, their comfortable Texas home, school, church, McDonald's, the backyard pool, his room. He remembered every song he had ever heard, every TV show, every friend, acquaintance, enemy, every passing face in the mall. He remembered the wallpaper. The flyspecks on it. Everything.

He dredged everything up out of his memory, everything, every fragment of everything. Memory was all he had. Memory and the unchanging tableau of the hibernation berth's lid, the wire mesh catwalk above it, the shadow of the berths stacked above his.

At some point, after a very long time, he began

to remember memories that were not his. The memories that belonged to the other sleepers became his as well. Real, imagined, or it made no difference?

He reached out with his mind, searching, desperate, like no human child had ever been desperate before; he strained to touch something new, anything that would feed the hunger. But the hunger was a bottomless pit, a gulf that could never be filled, a silence that could not be broken.

Real or unreal? he asked himself, wondered, then, after a while, stopped caring. Let any image come, he welcomed it. Let any new idea appear, it was a banquet, and he didn't care if it was real or unreal.

The years reeled by. He felt the deaths all around him. He felt the dim lights go out one by one. He felt all the awesome emptiness of space as the shuttle rode feeble light waves far, far beyond the orbit of dead Earth.

And when at last the new thing happened, the unexpected thing, the impossible thing, he still did not know if it was real.

The unexpected brought hope, and hope shattered him all over again.

Billy Weir lay still.

Waiting.

CHAPTER ONE

"IS ANYONE THERE?"

Jobs opened his eyes.

He closed them again, and slept.

More than a day later he opened his eyes again. Blinked. The blink seemed to last long minutes. His eyelids slid slowly, slowly up, and slowly, slowly down. Like rusty garage doors.

What he saw meant nothing. The rods and cones in his eyes sent messages down a nerve wire that responded as slowly as his lids. Nerve fired nerve in ludicrously slow motion.

When at last the images reached his brain they did not electrify his visual centers. The images seeped like a stain, transmitted reluctantly by rusty neurons.

Blink.

See.

Process.

But no one was yet at home in Jobs's brain. This slow-motion action was carried on automatically, mechanically. A very old car engine being started. Starter grinding. Crankshaft turning resentfully. No spark to light the gas.

Then, all at once, he was there.

He was there. Aware. Aware of being aware. Able to form a question. Able to wonder. To experience confusion.

Where was he?

For that matter, who was he?

His eyes scanned slowly, left to right, practically screeching in their sockets, ball bearings that had not been lubricated in far too long.

Something close. Partly clear, frosted over. And something beyond the partly clear partition. A wire mesh, just a couple of feet above his face.

He was on his back. Arms at his side.

Sebastian Andreeson. That was his name. Yes.

No. Jobs. That was the name he'd taken.

Jobs. Okay.

Now where was he? And why did he feel so awful?

He hurt. Everywhere. From fingernails to toenails and everything in between. His head hurt. Hurt like he'd caught a fastball in the temple.

His mouth hurt. Sandpaper and twigs.

His skin itself hurt, as if someone had removed it, stretched it out, and reattached it badly. It didn't seem to fit.

Where am I? he wondered, but no sound came out. He knew sound should have come out, but surely that dry, wispy rattle couldn't be the right sound.

He tried to move a hand.

Exquisite pain. Pain that made his breath catch in his throat, and that in itself hurt.

Still, he had to move. Painful or not, he had to find out what was going on. He couldn't just lie here. Wherever "here" was.

He was a little afraid. This wasn't right. This wasn't normal. Was it?

He searched his memory. Not like opening computer files. More like prying open the door to a cobwebbed library full of ancient crumbling p-books.

He tried again to move his hand. It still hurt. Nevertheless, he moved it, raised it slowly to touch his face. He touched his chin. Not very useful, but reassuring.

The other hand. *Move it, too. There you go, Jobs, both hands together. There you go. The release switch is right there.*

"How do I know?" he wondered aloud.

Doesn't matter how I know, he told himself, silently now, *I just know. The release for the hibernation berth . . .*

(3)

What? Hibernation berth?

Brain waking up. Door to memory open. Okay. Rest a minute.

Hibernation berth, we know that. Right?

Yes, Jobs, we know that.

Suddenly memory came pouring forth, a waterfall of memory, a drowning surge of memory. Mom — *Mayflower* — shuttle — asteroid — Mo'-Steel — solar sails — the Rock — the commander shooting himself — that crazy kid and his murdering brother and the Rock and oh, god, Cordelia, no, no, no, no, everyone smashed to pieces, Earth broken, broken, all those people dead —

"Ahh, ahhh!" he moaned.

His right hand found the release, pushed it, and the Plexiglas lid slid open halfway and stuck.

He pushed up, hard, both hands, agony!

Tried to sit up and failed. A vast weariness came over him. His head swam, and he slipped back and under, under, under.

Many hours later Jobs opened his eyes again.

He knew who he was and where he was. And even why he was there.

The Mayflower Project. Earth's pitiful, last-second reaction to annihilation. The asteroid everyone just called the Rock. Jobs had seen it hit. There had been problems deploying the solar sails, he and the pilot were the only ones conscious. So Jobs revived Mo'-Steel and the two of them had gone EVA to repair the problem. They had been out there, hanging in orbit, with a perfect, uncluttered view as the massive asteroid struck Earth and took seven billion lives.

He sat up. Carefully. Cautiously.

He stared at the hibernation berth next to his own. His dad's berth.

The Plexiglas was dark. The dull yellow lights showed something fibrous, as if the berth had been filled with . . .

Jobs reeled. His stomach heaved with nothing to expel. A weird moan came from his dry throat.

The berth was filled with what could only be fungus of some sort, generations of it, filling the berth. Like bread mold. That's how it looked. Green and black. No shape visible within, nothing human, just a six-foot box filled with decay.

Jobs's hands shook. He reached to open the lid.

No. No. No, he couldn't. No, there was nothing in there, nothing for him to see. Let it be an undifferentiated horror, don't let some faint outline of the familiar appear. He didn't want to see his father's skull, his teeth grinning up through the rot, no.

He turned away.

"Is anyone there?" he croaked.

No answer.

It took forever to roll out of the berth. He moved like the oldest man on Earth. He moved like some arthritic hundred-year-old. He panted, exhausted, on his knees, wedged between his own berth and his father's.

He crawled, gasping with exertion. His mother's berth. Oh, please, not that rotting filth. Anything but that.

He pulled himself to where he could look in, weeping without tears. His mother was still there. Her skin was crumpled parchment. Her eye sockets were sunken, eyes gone. Some of her teeth lay in a heap in the back of her throat. They had fallen from absent gums. A gold crown still gleamed.

Dead. No possible doubt. Dead. Dead for a long time, dead.

His brother? Edward?

He crawled to his brother's berth, and there, breathing peacefully, his brother rested, as though napping.

Jobs lay half-across his brother's berth and fell asleep.

(CHAPTER TWO)

"IF THIS IS A DREAM, IT'S THE MOTHER, FATHER, SISTER, AND BROTHER OF WEIRD."

"You're alive," a voice said.

A hand shook Jobs's shoulder, but gently, seemingly knowing the pain he was in.

Slowly he revived. He saw a half-ruined face. A pretty girl, Asian, with half her face melted like wax.

"You probably don't remember me," she said. "I'm 2Face. We met back on Earth. Do you remember Earth? Do you remember what happened?"

He nodded dully. He looked, helpless to stop himself, at the filthy decay of his father's berth.

"A lot are like that," 2Face said. "I don't think very many of us are still alive. On my way up here I saw a few who looked alive. Sleeping, still. And there are some that . . . some, I don't know."

Jobs searched her face. She looked as if she had been crying. But maybe that was because of the drooping eye on her burned side.

"Do you think you can walk?" 2Face asked.

"I don't know," Jobs said.

"I think maybe we should get out of here," 2Face said.

Jobs shook his head. "We have to help these . . ."

"We're too weak. I keep falling asleep. I just heard you, so I climbed up here. But we have to get out. Outside. This place is . . . there are dead people everywhere." Her voice that had been so calm was edging toward hysteria. "There's just things, people, stuff you don't, I mean, I was climbing up here because I heard you moving and I passed by . . . and my mom . . . it's just . . . and they don't even smell, you know, not like dead people, like nothing, or like, like yeast, like bread . . ."

"Take it easy, take it easy, don't think about it," Jobs said.

"Don't think about it?!" 2Face screamed. "Don't think about it?!"

Jobs grabbed her face in his hands. The melted flesh felt strange. She stared at him, wild.

"We start screaming, we're never going to stop," Jobs said. "My brain is ready to explode, my mom and dad and everything. But we have to think. We have to think."

She nodded vigorously, searching his eyes as if

looking for reflections of her own panic. "Okay, we stick together, okay?"

"Yeah," Jobs agreed readily. "We stick together. Help each other. Neither one of us thinks too much, okay? We just try and figure out . . ." He couldn't imagine what he had to figure out. The images of his parents, the fear that his little brother might awaken and see them for himself, all of it was too much, like he was trying to take a drink from a fire hose, too much data, too much horror.

2Face said, "Okay, come on, we stick together." Her calm had returned, almost as if it was her turn to be rational while he fought the torrent of fear and grief. "Okay, we need to find out what happened. Are we . . . I mean, where are we, the ship, I mean? Did we land somewhere? Are we still in space?"

"Yeah. Yeah." Jobs nodded, anxious to come to grips with simple problems. "Yeah. We're not weightless. Okay. We're not weightless. So we can't be in space. Unless we're accelerating. Then we'd have weight."

"That's good, think about that," 2Face said.

"Let's go up. To the bridge. We can see where we are."

"To the bridge. Maybe the captain is up there, he can tell us, if he made it, I mean."

"He didn't," Jobs said, remembering a dull thump, the sound of a gun being fired. The sound of a man's choice not to live on when his wife and children and home and very species were gone. "Long story. There were some problems. Come on. Let's go to the bridge."

Each step up the ladder was painful. But each step was less painful than the step before.

They climbed past the place where D-Caf and his brother, Mark Melman, had stowed away. Where Mark had shot the Marine sergeant. What was her name? Jobs couldn't remember. Had she survived? How could she, she'd been shot, badly wounded when they bundled her into a hibernation berth. His own perfectly healthy parents had not survived, how could a wounded woman?

And Mo'Steel. What about Mo? He should check on Mo.

No. No more hideous Plexiglas coffins. He didn't want to see any more horrors.

They reached the crawlway that connected the cargo area to the flight deck. The hatch was open. Jobs went in first.

He had to climb up. The tunnel was meant to be used either in a weightless environment or crawled through when the shuttle was at rest horizontally.

The tunnel opened onto a space below the flight deck. It was mostly crammed with lockers. What they contained he didn't know, but water would have been his first choice. He was desperately thirsty.

There was a ladder that in this position was more an impediment than a help. He crawled onto the flight deck. It was designed for horizontal flight, with the seats set in such a way that during the landing phase, the pilots would be positioned like the pilots of any commercial jet. So when Jobs entered the flight deck the seats were above him, over his back.

He stood up and stretched.

Looking straight up, Jobs could see a sliver of light through the small cockpit windshield. Like looking up through a skylight. Strange. The sky was blue, and for a moment he felt a leap of irrational hope. They were home! On Earth. All of it a dream.

But the blue of the sky was not the depthless, indeterminate blue of Earth's sky. The sky seemed to be made up of blue scales. Dabs of blue and dabs of violet. Even streaks of green. And the cloud he saw was no cloud that had ever floated through Earth's sky. It was white in parts, but also brown, with streaks of brown dragged across the white.

The whole mass of the sky moved, vibrated. As if

the wind blew, but blew nowhere in particular, just reshuffled the scales and smears of color.

"What is it?" 2Face asked. She was staring up past him.

"I don't know."

He helped her to her feet. They stood on what would normally be a vertical bulkhead.

The shuttle had landed. Somewhere. Gravity was downward, which meant that, impossible as it clearly was, it had landed nose up. It had landed in takeoff position. Utterly impossible.

The shuttle had no way to achieve this. The thought had been that the ship's computers would, on sensing the right circumstances, trim the solar sails to achieve deceleration and enter orbit around some theoretical, hoped-for, prayed-for planet.

After that, the thinking was that any orbit would inevitably deteriorate, and the shuttle would then be able to land in its normal configuration under the guidance of a revived pilot.

Of course, the shuttle normally landed on a smooth, paved runway. Not on prairie. Not on water. Not on mountainsides. Not in craters.

Jobs knew (just as everyone aboard knew) what a mishmash of faint hopes and ludicrous delusions this mission represented. There never had been anything more than a disappearingly small chance of success.

Fly through space toward no particular goal, have the solar sails work both to accelerate and decelerate and then have the absurd good luck to land on a planet with reasonable gravity and a very convenient landing strip positioned wherever they happened to touch down?

Absurd.

But to do all that and somehow end up *vertical*?

"Maybe we're still asleep," Jobs muttered.

"I don't think so, Duck. I don't have dreams like this."

The voice was instantly familiar.

"Mo?"

Mo'Steel leaned out into view overhead. He was perched in the captain's seat. He was smiling, but nothing like his usual Labrador-retriever grin.

"I'm alive," Mo'Steel reported. "If this is a dream, it's the mother, father, sister, and brother of weird. We got all of weird's cousins in on this. Come on up. You gotta see this. You have *got* to see this."

(CHAPTER THREE)

"OKAY, THIS IS NOT CERTIFIED ORGANIC. THIS IS MESSED UP."

It took some effort but 2Face managed to climb up to where Mo'Steel sat. He took her hands and hauled her up by main force. He was amazingly strong, especially given the weak-kitten state she and Jobs were in. He must have been awake longer. He seemed more fully recovered from hibernation.

Once up, 2Face helped Mo'Steel pull Jobs up to their now-cramped spot. They squeezed together onto the back-support of the copilot's chair, with their heads pushed into gray panels of switches and knobs and LEDs.

Mo'Steel nodded toward the other seat. A space suit was strapped in place minus helmet. A skull lolled against the collar.

"The commander," Jobs said. To 2Face he explained, "He decided he didn't want to come."

"Yeah," Mo'Steel said.

2Face stared. It was almost comical. A grinning Halloween skeleton dressed up as an astronaut. Surely it had been there a long time. She tore her eyes away, unwilling to think about it. Her mother was dead. She had no grief to spare for this poor man.

Mo'Steel said, "If you stand up you can look out and around through the side window here. Careful, though, it takes a while before the old body gets hooked up right. And watch this panel here, sharp edges."

Jobs stood. 2Face stood, held on to what should have been an overhead array of switches. She looked.

She gasped.

The ship stood tall, the only man-made thing. Filling the narrow view was a landscape that seemed to literally vibrate with color and movement. Green and yellow and blue. There were trees with royal-blue trunks and branches, brown trunks, even purple. Leaves that were more like rough smears of color, light and dark greens, honey-golds. The branches seemed to poke in and out of the leaves with only the most rudimentary logic.

Tall grass, or at least something that at first glance looked like grass, extended down a hill to a blue-and-violet river bordered in umber.

Beyond the river the grass took over again, off-set by a smear of reddish-brown.

In the distance was the suggestion of a village, whitewashed walls tinged green and red tile roofs set at improbable angles.

Above it all, the pulsating blue sky, so alive, but at the same time flat, without depth.

"Excellent, huh?" Mo'Steel asked.

"What is it?" 2Face wondered aloud. "None of it seems real. I mean, I think it's real, but it's like . . . I don't know. I don't know how to explain it. I mean, the sky, it's as if the blue isn't air but a million small blue birds flying around all packed in close to-gether."

"It's beautiful," Jobs said. "The colors are so intense. How can it be real, though? Look at the way the river moves. Shouldn't water move like water, no matter where you are? It's more like . . . like it kind of smears past, like, like big sections of it kind of move together."

"Maybe it's ice. Maybe it's not water at all," 2Face suggested.

"Or maybe our heads are all messed up," Mo'-Steel suggested. "You know? How long were we asleep? You know your eyes don't totally focus when you first wake up and stuff sounds too loud and all?"

2Face tore her gaze from the agitated, too-bright landscape. "Maybe you're right. Maybe it's all in our heads."

"This ship is standing upright," Jobs said cautiously. "That's impossible. Unless it's real, I mean. But theoretically it's impossible. So maybe this is just a dream."

"Deep," Mo'Steel mocked.

"Maybe my mom isn't dead," 2Face whispered. "Maybe none of them are dead. If it's a dream. We don't know, right?"

The three of them sat down, wedged uncomfortably together, hugging to keep from falling, sharing one seat until Mo'Steel leaped the gap to reach the chair occupied by the skeleton. "We're going to need to bury him, I guess."

"No hurry," Jobs said darkly.

Mo'Steel pulled at the seat belt but it came apart in his fingers. The corpse shifted, slid, fell off the side of the chair, fell to the bulkhead with a sound like a dropped bundle of sticks.

"Sorry, Commander," Mo'Steel said without seeming very disturbed. "What are we going to do?" Mo'Steel asked Jobs, sounding to 2Face as if it couldn't possibly be his responsibility to figure it out himself.

2Face wasn't sure she liked him. She was drawn to Jobs's quiet, thoughtful way. But Mo'Steel had a way of being jumpy in his own skin, like there were too many calories being burned. He reminded her of the landscape she'd just observed.

"I guess sooner or later we need to go back downstairs," Jobs said. His reluctance was evident in his look and tone. He didn't try to hide the fact that what was down there in the *Mayflower* capsule horrified him.

2Face definitely shared that sense of horror. Pain was down there. Loss. Unimaginable loss.

Mo'Steel rocked back and forth on his heels and looked like he'd rather talk about something else. He stood up and looked out of the port-side window and yelped.

"Yah-ah-ah!" He pulled back, blinked, looked again. He pointed accusingly. "Okay, this is not certified organic. This is messed up."

"We've seen it," 2Face said, feeling a little annoyed.

"Uh-uh." Mo'Steel shook his head vigorously. He pointed at the starboard-side window. "You've seen *that*. You have *not* seen *this*."

Jobs frowned and with help from his friend made his way across to the far seat. He took a long look, several breaths, and took 2Face's hand to guide her across.

She pushed between the two guys and looked. No, she had not seen this.

It was in black-and-white. Entirely. Not a splash of color, not a glimmer. The sky was gray with puffy white clouds. The ground was broken up into a series of deep channels or canyons cut deep around precarious mesas. Looming in the distance, rising up from the fractured plain was a massive mountain range, snowcapped at the jagged peaks.

No color. None. Light gray and medium gray and darkest gray shadows edging to black in the deep places.

They raced back at dangerous speeds to check the first view. It was still there, still a wild profusion of greens and blues and golds.

Two landscapes. Completely incompatible. Completely impossible.

"The dream thing is seeming more and more likely," 2Face said.

"There should be a chronometer of some kind," Jobs said suddenly. He began searching the ranks of dials, readouts, and switches. Most of the readouts were blank. But when he toggled certain switches some of the readouts came to life.

"There should be some kind of mission clock," he muttered. "Time from launch or whatever. There. There it is."

A small digital readout displayed a long string of numbers.

"It's still running. Look. Not seconds, minutes. It's only showing minutes," 2Face said, looking over his shoulder.

"Two-hundred-sixty-two million, eight-hundred-seventeen thousand, nine-hundred-and-twelve minutes," Jobs said. "Mo?"

To 2Face's amazement Mo'Steel calculated instantaneously.

"Five-hundred years, twelve days, and some spare change, Duck," Mo'Steel said.

(CHAPTER FOUR)

"WE HAVE TO DO WHAT WE CAN."

As they descended into the capsule again, Jobs was grateful for the mysterious landscape of the planet. Grateful for the mystery of how the shuttle carrying the *Mayflower* capsule had come to land in so impossible a position. Anything that took his mind off the work at hand was welcome.

His father and mother were dead. If his brother, Edward, was still alive at all, he was unconscious.

Five centuries. They had drifted through space for five-hundred years. Not strange that the untested hibernation equipment had failed his parents, more surprising that it had preserved him. Nothing man-made worked for five hundred years.

Another mystery. More unknowns. So much better than the knowns.

"I don't think we'd better open any of these units," Jobs said. "Even if we see someone we think is alive, we better let them be. I don't understand how this system works. But it must have a pro-grammed revival sequence."

"I hear something," 2Face said. "Listen."

Jobs heard it, too. A human voice. Groaning.

Mo'Steel scrambled into the "basement," through the hatch and then down the circular steps as fast as a monkey, sliding more than stepping.

"Someone's alive down here," he called up.

Jobs and 2Face followed at a more normal pace.

"How did he do that?" 2Face whispered. "The thing with the minutes, I mean."

In a low voice Jobs said, "Mo's crazy, he's a wild man, doesn't care about much except the next adrenaline rush. Doesn't mean he's stupid, especially with numbers."

"Idiot savant," 2Face muttered.

"Mo's my best friend," Jobs said. He would have said more, but Mo'Steel didn't need defending. If 2Face was as smart as she seemed, she'd come to ap-preciate Mo'Steel. If not, well, that would be her loss.

"Sorry," 2Face said.

They reached the level where Mo'Steel squatted beside a young woman. Jobs recognized the Marine sergeant. Her uniform, like his own clothing, was brittle and in tatters, but the dark camouflage pattern was still recognizable.

She was not alone in her berth. A child lay there, a boy, seemingly asleep on her belly. It wasn't a newborn. It might have been a two- or three-year-old. And there was a weird, cylindrical, almost translucent piece of skin that seemed to hold them together. It began near the sergeant's shoulder and snaked its way into the baby's side.

Tamara was awake. Confused, as Jobs had been on waking, sleepy.

"Take it easy, take it easy," Mo'Steel comforted her in a gentle voice. "No rush. You're not going anywhere yet."

The woman blinked and tried to focus. She tried to speak but only a groan was heard.

2Face leaned over. "You're on the shuttle still. We've landed. Somewhere. We don't know where."

Jobs pointed to a small round hole in the woman's uniform near where the long, cordlike piece of skin started, and gave 2Face a significant look.

2Face tugged gently at the cloth. It tore easily. The bullet hole in her shoulder could be clearly seen as a neat round scar, lighter than the surrounding flesh.

Tamara seemed to be trying to form a question.

"You were shot. You may not remember it right away," Jobs said. "A stowaway shot you. But it looks like it healed during hibernation. Maybe the machine . . . maybe just time . . ."

"No," Tamara said, forcing the word out. "Baby . . . my baby . . ."

"She must have been pregnant when she went into hibernation," 2Face said in a low voice. Then, loud enough for Tamara to hear, "The baby was born. God knows how. It's right here. It's on you. In fact, it's attached to you."

Tamara nodded slowly. Her hands felt blindly and Mo'Steel gently guided her fingers to her baby's face.

The baby opened its eyes. Jobs recoiled, banged his head on the low deck above. 2Face cried out, an expression of pure horror.

The baby's eyes had run, liquid, out onto its mother's belly. It stared at them now with empty eye sockets.

"Wha . . .?" Tamara moaned.

Mo'Steel was the first to recover. "Nothing. Nothing, lady. Don't worry, it's okay."

Tamara slipped back into sleep. The baby, at any

rate, blinked its empty eyes and seemed to be watching them with great interest.

Jobs, 2Face, and Mo'Steel pulled back.

"Radiation," Jobs whispered. "Five centuries in space. This capsule is lead-lined, but five-hundred years of hard radiation while the kid is slowly, slowly somehow growing and, I mean, during cell division and all . . ." He stopped, unable to speak. He felt like a mountain was falling on him. Like a man standing on the beach as a tidal wave hits. He was being buried alive, smothered, crushed.

Way too much.

Jobs felt Mo'Steel's hand on his shoulder.

"It's woolly, Duck, but you gotta strap it up and keep moving. We can't go all slasher chick and start screaming. There's weirder stuff than this coming."

Jobs nodded, but he wanted very badly to punch his friend in the face. He didn't want to be comforted, let alone be told he had to be a good soldier and get on with his life. He wanted to cry. He wanted to scream. He wanted to wake up and not be here. It was too much, too much. Impossible to process a tenth of it, a billionth of it.

His hands were shaking. A result of the hibernation? No. A result of waking up and seeing.

"We need to get some kind of grip on things here," 2Face said. "Let's check every berth. Let's see what's what. How about that? One by one, bottom to top, okay?"

"What she said," Mo'Steel agreed. He was looking very earnestly at his friend.

Jobs covered his face with his hands. "As far as I know we have no food. No water. We've probably all taken a hundred lifetimes' worth of radiation. I don't know what that is outside there on the planet, but it can't be natural. Maybe no air outside. My folks are dead. Yours, too, mostly. The whole human race is dead. Maybe just the three of us and . . . and that woman and some kind of mutant alien baby."

"Yeah. Like I said, very woolly."

2Face said, "Jobs, you said yourself: It can't be. The planet out there, the ship standing this way. It can't be. Not unless there's something else."

"Yeah?"

"So, what's the something else, Jobs? Don't you want to find out?"

He laughed bitterly. "You're trying to appeal to my curiosity?"

"We have to do what we can," 2Face said. "You're right, the human race is all over. Except for us. Me, I'm not going to roll over and die. You want to give up, Jobs, I can't stop you, I guess, but I have to try. We're *it*, however many of us are alive on this stupid ship. That's not why we should give up, that's why we can't give up."

"Well, good luck, Eve, go forth and multiply," Jobs snapped.

2Face started to answer back, but Jobs saw Mo'Steel take her arm and shake his head. "He's coming around."

Jobs glared at his friend. "You think you know me, don't you, Mo?"

"Yeah, 'migo, I know you. There's some deep stuff to figure out here. You can't leave it alone. I know you pretty good, Duck: You can't leave it alone."

Jobs nodded dully. He looked up at 2Face. The smooth half of her face was set, determined. The burned side, with its drooping eye, seemed to weep. *There was a poem in there somewhere,* Jobs thought.

He should formulate a plan. He should step up and try to figure it all out. But right now the strength wasn't in him.

"Lead on," he said to 2Face.

(CHAPTER FIVE)

"YOU DON'T WANT TO SEE."

It had taken . . . how long so far? 2Face had no way of knowing. No watch, no clock, maybe no need for them.

It was taking a long time as time is experienced — subjectively. Time dragged when it was measured out in hideous deaths and uncertain lives.

And then there was the thirst. She wanted water. Needed it, and soon. And they had no idea where even to begin looking.

So they kept up the grim task of accounting.

Of the Eighty who had originally been chosen to fly on the *Mayflower* Project, one had died in the riot on the ground. His berth had been taken by Tamara Hoyle, who had been shot — but not killed — by the stowaway Mark Melman who had, in turn, been killed.

The mission copilot had been killed by D-Caf Melman. D-Caf had been given the hibernation berth belonging to the man he had killed. The mission commander had taken his life into his own hands.

So seventy-nine people had entered hibernation. Of those, they had already confirmed twenty-one who were very definitely dead. Thus far 2Face had counted nineteen, plus Tamara's "child," who were either alive and active or in various states of revival.

Among the confirmed dead were both of Jobs's parents, Mo'Steel's father, and 2Face's mother. Older people had fared worse. Some adults had made it, like Mo'Steel's mother and 2Face's father and even Tamara Hoyle.

They climbed up a level.

"Cheese," Mo'Steel reported, checking the first berth. It was the shorthand term for the death that Jobs's father had died. A death that filled the berth with green–black mold.

"Cheese" for the moldy ones. "Crater" for the ones, like one young girl, who had been killed by micrometeorites. And "facelift" for the ones who had been dried out, stretched, were nothing but parchment skin over skeletons.

It was brutal jargon for a brutal job. They were

protecting themselves, 2Face knew. They couldn't weep for each death. There were seven billion dead.

"Oh, god." Jobs recoiled from the next berth.

"What?" 2Face asked. She was still worried about him. She didn't know if he was a strong person who had suffered a moment of weakness, or a weak person. They needed strength.

"You don't want to see," Jobs said.

2Face hesitated. But no, she couldn't start giving in to the fear now. She pressed past Jobs and looked. A man. His body looked like a target, like he'd been shot full of holes, bloodless holes. Something had burrowed tunnels, some as small as a quarter inch in diameter, some three times as big, in every exposed inch of flesh. He was dried out like so many of the others, mummified. But none of the others had been eaten alive like this.

Jobs wiped his face with his hands. He looked sick. But then, 2Face supposed she did, too. This was vile work.

Beside the worm-eaten man was a girl in the early stages of revival. 2Face had met her in passing, just yesterday. Just yesterday five-hundred years ago. A "Jane." Not 2Face's kind of girl at all. But what could silly school cliques possibly matter now? She spoke some calming words to the girl, who fell back asleep.

"This one's alive, too," Mo'Steel reported from across the aisle.

The occupant of the berth was a kid, maybe twelve years old. Maybe younger. Or maybe he was just small for his age. He had dark, deep, almost sunken eyes. His skin was pale as death, so fragile you could see individual veins in his arms and face. His hair was black.

His eyes were open, staring, as blank as a doll's eyes.

"I know that kid," Jobs said. "His name's Billy. Billy something. Weir. Billy Weir?"

"Weird? Billy Weird? Needs to think about picking a new name," Mo'Steel said.

Jobs leaned in and said, "Billy. Billy. You were right: I'm here."

2Face exchanged a surprised look with Mo'Steel.

"Before we left, back at the barracks. He was walking in his sleep," Jobs said. "Talking. I think he was asleep, anyway. He said, 'You'll be there.' He said that to me."

"Billy, wake up, man," Mo'Steel said.

No response.

"Are we sure he's alive?" 2Face wondered.

"He's alive," Jobs said. "He's alive. It takes a while."

"His eyes are wide open. But he's not focusing at all."

"He's breathing."

2Face covered Billy's eyes with her hand, then removed it. She watched the pupils closely. They had widened in the dark and were now contracting in the light. "Okay, he's alive."

"Hey," a voice called. "Hey. Hey!"

"A live one," Mo'Steel remarked. "Up there. Come on. Old Billy here is not a morning person. Give the boy some time. Let's go see who's yelling."

2Face agreed. But Jobs would not stop staring at the impassive face of Billy Weir.

"Come on, Jobs," she said. "We'll come back."

"He said I'd be here," Jobs said.

"Yeah. Come on."

"That's a total of . . ." 2Face hesitated.

"Start with eighty including the baby," Mo'Steel said. "Looks like thirty-four alive or at least look alive. Forty-six . . . otherwise. You want the percent? Forty-two-point-five percent made it. Fifty-seven-point-five percent passed on."

"So far," 2Face said.

CHAPTER SIX

"ARE WE THERE YET?"

Billy Weir's eyes saw. His brain processed. But all at a glacial pace.

The faces were gone almost before he could take notice of their presence.

He was still taking note of the ship's landing. That, too, had happened too quickly to notice.

Had they ever really been there, those faces?

There.

More.

Faces.

Gone.

Fast as hummingbird's wings. The faces darted into view and disappeared. Impossible to recognize. Impossible when they moved so fast.

More?

Gone.

He wished they would slow down so he could

see them. He wished they would stay long enough for him to be sure they were real.

He heard a buzzing sound. Like bees, but only for a split second.

Silence returned. The silence he knew.

The silence he had listened to for five-hundred years.

It was unfair now, not to know, unfair. Or perhaps unreal.

Once before he'd thought he'd seen faces, impossible faces. Once before he'd thought he had heard voices. But those voices had hurt.

He remembered the pain. He had welcomed the pain, blessed the pain. It was something. Something in the valley of nothing. Pain meant life.

Those faces, these faces, they were real, weren't they?

Are we there? he wondered. *Are we there yet?*

CHAPTER SEVEN

"SUFFOCATE IN HERE OR SUFFOCATE OUT THERE. TAKE YOUR CHOICE."

Yago had a headache that would have killed a lesser person. He wanted a couple of aspirin and a glass of chilled spring water, possibly with a slice of lemon. But that was not happening.

The first thing he'd focused on after waking up was the creepy face of the femme who'd breezed him back into the world. That was no way to wake up.

2Face, that was her name.

He'd fallen back to sleep, and when he revived again it was Jobs he saw first, and that monkey-boy friend of his, and then some old guy named Errol Smith, and a woman named Connie Huerta who said she was a doctor although it turned out she was an obstetrician and didn't even have a Raleeve or an aspirin with her, which was not all that helpful.

And as Yago regained full consciousness others

came by to offer help or just stare balefully. Some weepy dope who was apparently 2Face's father from the way he kept boo-hooing at her. And then there was a "Jane" who called herself Miss Blake. At least she was nice-looking, not some half-nightmare like 2Face.

For some strange reason 2Face seemed to be the one handing out orders. Her dad, Shy Hwang, and Errol and the doctor, as the only revived adults, should have been the ones to assume command, but none of the three seemed to be up for it. So, somehow, it was 2Face the freak chick who was making the calls, and so far Yago, who was feeling like a squashed bug as he climbed, rickety as a three-legged chair, from his berth, had decided to play along.

The plan was to get out of the *Mayflower*, which was fine as far as he was concerned. He suffered from a touch of claustrophobia — many great men did. Jobs had said something about the external environment being very bizarre.

"As long as there's air," Yago had said.

"We don't know that," Jobs answered.

"Um, what?"

Jobs had shrugged and explained in a distracted way that it didn't really matter much since now that they were off hibernation the air in the *Mayflower* couldn't last for long. "Suffocate in here or suffocate out there," he'd muttered. "Take your choice."

Fortunately Yago was too dopey still to experience the full-fledged panic that usually followed the word *suffocate*.

"Strap it up," he told himself. "Keep it together. Be out soon. There's going to be air. You didn't come all this way to suck vacuum."

Of course, there was the question of how exactly they were going to get out. Jobs and Errol, busy little tool-jockeys, were evidently already at work on the problem and managed to open the cargo bay doors of the shuttle. Which was fine, but it turned out no one had ever considered the possibility that the ship would land vertically. The whole idea had been that the ship would land horizontally, like it was supposed to do. Then the hibernation berths would open and the people would simply step out and promptly fall any number of feet to the nearest external bulkhead, then, having survived those injuries, would crawl to the only exit door.

Idiots.

"We don't have a way out?" Yago asked in a shrill voice.

"They were in a hurry putting this mission together," Jobs said in defense of the NASA people. "To be honest with you, I don't think they really considered there was much to worry about. We weren't going anywhere."

Yago felt a surge of rage, rage at stupidity. He hated stupidity. Hated having to tolerate it, hated having to bite his tongue and swallow the bile. But, by god, if they weren't already dead along with the rest of *H. sapiens,* he'd like to find a way to hurt the NASA clowns who'd put this fiasco together.

And yet, he was alive. Alive and seething. It reassured him. Anger was an attribute of the living.

"I have to get out of here," Yago said.

"Yeah. We all do."

Yago had relapsed back into his berth, too groggy to argue. And some time later he saw Mo'-Steel and Jobs come huffing and puffing up the ladder carrying an inert but apparently conscious kid. Jobs kept talking to him.

"We're there, Billy. We're there."

That was okay, but it was the next person to climb past that brought Yago up and fully awake with a jolt. A young black woman cradling a great big baby. The baby stared right at Yago with cavernous eye sockets. And no eyeballs.

"Okay, I'm awake," Yago said.

He began to climb after the others.

Up and up. Past berth after berth of stomach-roiling death. He hoped no one was going to open some of those berths. The smell would probably be fatal all by itself.

As he climbed, he kept a rough count, anything to avoid thinking about the cramped, crowded, airless . . .

Maybe forty percent had died, he estimated, weighted toward older passengers. Good. The fewer adults he had to contend with, the better. He could deal with the likes of 2Face and Jobs. Adults would be tougher to manipulate and eventually control, though useful in the short run.

There was no doubt of the final outcome: Yago would rule these pitiful remnants of humanity. But first, he needed air. Hard to take over a world without air. Kind of pointless.

He reached the narrow platform just inside the external hatch. The dozen people so far revived crowded close together, crammed on the platform and on the nearest stairs. Yago strained to keep away from the eerie baby and to get close to Miss Blake. Being a Jane, she'd be easy to cow.

"Okay, are we all agreed we open the door?" 2Face asked.

Suddenly she was taking a vote? That was weak. A *leader should lead,* Yago observed. But a rather larger part of his mind was taken up with controlling the claustrophobic panic that kept threatening to boil over and result in shrill screaming and wild thrashing.

Couldn't do that. Couldn't panic.

Everyone agreed to open the door. Yago suspected he was not the only one unnaturally eager to push that door open.

2Face nodded. Jobs set down the blank-faced, wide-eyed Billy Weir and worked the lever.

Impossible not to hold your breath. Pointless, Yago realized, but impossible to resist. The air outside could be sulfuric acid. Or there could be no air at all.

Jobs swung the door open.

No air rushed out of the *Mayflower.*

No sulfuric acid rushed in.

Yago breathed. Held it. Breathed again.

Suddenly the baby began to chuckle.

That sound, added to the tension of remaining a second longer in this space-going mausoleum, snapped something in Yago.

"Move!" he shouted.

He pushed past the doctor, elbowed Miss Blake aside, and all at once hung at the edge of a precipice. The shuttle's cargo doors were open, exposing the lead-lined *Mayflower* capsule to eerie sunlight. It was a straight drop down the dull metal capsule, a straight drop down to a crash against the back wall of the shuttle's cargo bay.

Yago windmilled his arms, trying to cancel momentum. The doctor grabbed the back of his shirt but the rotten fabric tore away.

Yago fell forward, screaming.

Mo'Steel's arm shot out and caught Yago's spring-green hair. He pulled Yago back inside and sat him down with his legs dangling.

"When you're right on the edge like that, you don't want to windmill, and you don't want to go all spasmoid, you want to sit down," Mo'Steel advised. "Use your heels, bend at the knees, move your butt back, and sit down. It'll bruise your butt but that's a lot better than falling."

"Shut up!" Yago snapped.

Yago stared at the landscape, panting, and wondering how his body could still produce sweat, as dehydrated as he was.

The view was overwhelming. *Overwhelming*. Too

much color on the one side, too little on the other. The shuttle stood perfectly on the dividing line between the two environments.

Yago's first thought was that it was all an optical illusion. A picture. But he could feel the awesome depths of the gray-shade canyons to one side, and feel, too, the restless movement in the greens and golds and blues and pinks on the other side.

He glanced up at the sky. He had to close his eyes. The sky was similarly divided, all in blue with flat-looking clouds with brown-purple edges on one side, gray on gray over the canyon.

The survivors were all silent, staring.

"What is it?" Errol asked.

"Artificial," Jobs said. "Has to be. Nothing evolves naturally like this. This can't be the natural state of this planet."

Shy Hwang said, "Maybe it's not real. Maybe . . . I mean, maybe we're dead. Maybe we're all dead."

Yago snorted in derision. "Yeah, maybe it's heaven. Right. We flew to heaven on a magic shuttle full of dead people."

"The air seems breathable," a woman said. "Of course, there's no way to know what the nitrogen-oxygen-CO_2 ratio is, or what trace gases may be present."

Yago, with his junior politician's memory for names, remembered her as Olga Gonzalez, Mo'-Steel's mother. What was her job? Something scientific, no doubt — most of the Eighty had been NASA or NASA contractors.

"How do we get down?" 2Face asked.

The Marine with the unsettling baby in her arms stepped forward to get a better look down. "Spot me," she said to Mo'Steel.

Mo'Steel put a sort of loose half nelson on her and two others in turn held Mo'Steel. Tamara Hoyle looked down at the drop, at least forty feet. She stepped back.

"Rope is out. First of all, I don't think there's any aboard, and second — judging by the way our clothes have rotted — even if there was, we'd never be able to trust it. But there should be plenty of wire on this ship. We braid it together and make a cable."

"We can't go ripping wire out of the ship," Errol protested. "This ship is all we have."

"This ship is never going to fly again," Olga Gonzalez said.

"This ship is all we have," Jobs said. "But we should be able to safely harvest wire from the hibernation berths that have failed."

"Good. Let's do that," 2Face said.

And again Yago grated at her assumption of authority. Who was she to be making decisions? But now was maybe not the time for a fight. Although now was definitely the time to start looking at options. Surely one of these adults could be manipulated into pushing 2Face aside.

Yago surveyed the disturbing landscape. Maybe it wasn't much of a kingdom, but it was going to be his.

CHAPTER EIGHT

"USUALLY THERE'S NO PAIN, BUT THIS MAY BE DIFFERENT."

It took hours and Mo'Steel was growing ever more impatient. He assumed he'd be the first person down the wire, and he was totally adrenal. Slippy-sliding down a wire to be the first person to step foot on a new planet, that was exalted.

Besides, he had to get away from his mom. She kept bursting into tears over his dad and over the whole world and all. Mo'Steel had loved his dad, but he lived by the creed of no regrets. Sooner or later you were going to miss your grip on the world, you were going to push the limit too far, and Mother G. would grab you, run you up to terminal velocity, and squash you flat.

True, it wasn't gravity that had killed his dad. But, Mother G. or whatever, the principle was the same: Sooner or later they canceled your account, had to happen, no point in boo-hooing over it. It was the deal, if you wanted the rush of the big ride you had to accept the fact that every ride comes to an end.

Still, he would miss his dad. He'd gone to cheese, and Mo'Steel regretted seeing him that way. He regretted that memory maybe squeezing out the good stuff his dad had been.

"Come here, I need your help."

It was the doctor. Mo'Steel glanced at Jobs to see whether his friend needed him, but Jobs was underneath one of the berths working away at removing wire and optical cable.

"All yours, Doc," Mo'Steel said.

He stepped over a prone and still-staring Billy Weir, then climbed down the ladder to a berth where the doctor had laid Tamara Hoyle and her baby.

"You don't faint at the sight of blood, do you?" the doc asked.

Mo'Steel laughed. "I've seen my own bones poking out through my own skin and didn't faint," Mo'-Steel answered. It was something he was proud of. He was the Man of Steel, with more titanium and petri-dish replacement parts than the whole rest of his class put together.

The doctor nodded. "Okay. How about bashful? You're not going to go all giggly, right?"

Mo'Steel frowned. What did she mean? Then he

looked at Tamara Hoyle and her baby. And the weird piece of skin that kept them attached.

He swallowed hard and tried not to lose his balance. Blood was one thing. This was different.

"Uh, maybe you need to get, like, one of the femmes," Mo'Steel protested.

"I tried. That girl, the one in the frilly dress and the antique shoes? What's her name? Miss Blake? She agreed to help, but I don't think she's physically strong enough. 2Face is stronger, but she's busy and your mom, she's . . . she's upset. I need someone steady."

"Okay," Mo'Steel moaned. "Okay. Okay. I can do it."

She drew Mo'Steel close and spoke in a whisper. "My surgical steel instruments are in decent shape, but I have no bandages, they're all decayed. I don't have a lot of confidence in any of my topicals; I don't know what five centuries does to antibiotics or antivirals. I don't even have soap or water. And I don't have any idea what kind of shape our immune systems are in. But the thing I need you for is that this umbilical cord — if that's what this is — is not normal. Usually there's no pain, but this may be different. I need you to be ready to take hold of the sergeant in the event she begins to move around. Can you do that?"

Mo'Steel nodded, not trusting his dust-dry mouth to form an answer.

"Okay, Sergeant Hoyle — Tamara," Dr. Huerta said to her patient, "this shouldn't be any problem at all. If you feel any discomfort, just let me know."

"I'm okay," Tamara said. She stroked the baby's head.

The baby opened its empty eyes and yawned. Mo'Steel saw a mouth full of tiny white teeth.

Good thing they had a doctor. She could deal with the baby. The baby scared Mo'Steel. Doctors were used to that stuff. Used to giant, silent, eyeless babies.

Right.

Doctor Huerta took up position at bedside, kneeling over the young woman. Mo'Steel squatted behind Tamara's head, arms akimbo, ready to make a grab.

Doctor Huerta retrieved a piece of fiber-optic cable Jobs must have given her and began to cinch it around the cord, two inches from the baby's side.

The baby turned its head sharply to look at her.

Doctor Huerta began tying off the cord close to the mother's shoulder. Mo'Steel looked studiously away, suddenly fascinated by the bulkhead.

The baby stirred and a low, animal moan came from its mother.

"Did you feel that?" the doctor asked her. She held the scalpel poised in her hand, ready for the first cut.

Suddenly the baby lunged. Its chubby fist grabbed for the scalpel. Doctor Huerta yanked it away.

The baby bared its teeth in a dangerous scowl and, as Mo'Steel watched in growing horror, his mother's face mirrored the expression.

Tamara made her own grab for the scalpel and caught the doctor's wrist. The doctor lost her balance and Tamara let her fall.

Mo'Steel yelled, "Help! Help down here!"

The doctor fell straight back, hitting her head on the edge of the berth. The scalpel flew from her hand. Mo'Steel lunged for the doctor but he was awkwardly positioned and now, as he tried to lean over Tamara, the baby was clawing feebly at his chest and neck.

It didn't take long to realize that the doctor was not moving. Wasn't breathing.

"Help! Someone help me down here!"

Mo'Steel coiled his legs and leaped across Tamara, hit his head on the deck, and came up, brain swimming, swirling. The doctor was still. He fished for the scalpel but was knocked violently off-balance by a kick from Tamara.

He went facedown and the Marine was on him. They struggled, shoving and pushing to find the scalpel.

Jobs appeared, tumbling down the stairs. He stepped on the scalpel just as Tamara touched it with outstretched fingers.

"Cut the cord!" Mo'Steel yelled. He yanked Tamara back with all his strength. He was strong, but the whipcord Marine sergeant was stronger. Her hands closed around his throat and already he was seeing double as she stopped the flow of blood to his brain.

Jobs knelt, picked up the scalpel. He made a quick, slashing cut, severed the cord, and instantly the death grip on Mo'Steel's throat loosened.

Mo'Steel pushed Tamara back and slid out from under her.

The Marine sat up, then bent forward and began vomiting. The baby lay on its back, gasping, staring blindly.

More people arrived, running to respond to Mo'Steel's earlier cries.

Too late. Way too late. The doctor was dead.

CHAPTER NINE

"WE DIDN'T LAND. WE WERE CAPTURED."

Miss Violet Blake's mother was alive. Her father was not.

Violet had seen her father, and the image had been burned so deeply into her thoughts that she could not imagine ever closing her eyes again without seeing his poor face disfigured by those countless holes.

A hideous death. More horrible for her than for him, perhaps. He would have been, should have been, unconscious when the thing happened to him.

She prayed he'd been unconscious.

So many dead. A world dead. And now, new death, murder even, perhaps. Some said the Marine sergeant, Tamara Hoyle, had struck blindly, a panic reaction in part caused by the confusion of waking from a five-century nap. Mo'Steel said no, it had been deliberate. The woman herself, the sergeant, said nothing and no one had yet questioned her.

What would Violet say to her mother when she awoke? How could she console her? She had never been close to her mother. Wylson Lefkowitz-Blake was her daughter's polar opposite. An entrepreneur, a businesswoman who had built the software giant Wyllco Inc. from scratch, starting with three employees and some aging tablet computers. Her signature software *RemSleep 009* had made Wylson Lefkowitz-Blake a billionaire. And it had made her indispensable to NASA.

It would have been easier for Violet Blake if her father had been the one to survive. She'd always been her daddy's little girl. It was her father who had first introduced her to art, to serious music, to literature. It was her father who had given her *Pride and Prejudice,* and it was there, in the mannerly, elegant, understated, and unhurried world of Jane Austen that Violet had found her place in the world.

Violet was a freak in the world of school, because to reject a world dominated by soulless technology, a world where no thought ever seemed to go unspoken, where no feeling went unexpressed, a world devoid of *politesse,* a world without delicacy or tact, to reject that world was seen as unnatural, perhaps even dangerous. When she refused to wear a link even her teachers turned on her, demanding to know how she could stand being so "out of touch."

Violet had felt wrong growing up, wrong deep down in her soul. And she'd gone on feeling wrong till she found other girls like herself, girls who wanted to be *girls*. The frilly dresses and carefully piled hair were just the outward signs of a much deeper sense that the world had conspired to deprive girls of a unique *girlness*, and to deprive everyone of privacy, peace, contemplation.

It wasn't about playacting. Miss Blake knew she was not living in early-nineteenth-century England. Unlike some Janes, she did not attempt to copy the speech patterns of Austen characters. And it was not about being passive or witless. On the contrary, Austen's heroines were strong, determined, unafraid to make judgments or to express opinions.

Violet loved art. She enjoyed simple rituals. She enjoyed conversation. She enjoyed silence. And none of that found a place in the world of 2011.

Her father had understood immediately. Her mother had laughed at her, first in disbelief, then with outright contempt.

"Well, congratulations, Dallas," her mother told her once, "you've finally found the way to take a shot at me. I guess every teenager has to go through a phase like this."

"Mom, I am just trying to live my own life," Violet had responded. "And I would consider it a kindness if you would call me by my chosen name: Miss Blake."

"Miss Blake? Good lord. What's that? First name 'Miss'?"

"Dallas is not a name that pleases me. And the one great advantage of this day and age is that everyone feels free to change their name. I've chosen Violet as my first name. Violet Blake. You can call me Violet, but I'd prefer Miss Blake."

"Violet? Your name is Dallas. It has meaning. It's the city where you were born."

"And with each use of that name I am reminded of an event that I don't even remember!"

"That's not the point. I remember, and it's an important memory. You're my only daughter. Don't you understand what I'm saying?"

"Yes, Mother, I do. I *always* do," she'd answered, but of course the insult was lost on her mother.

Her father had comforted her. He had called her Violet.

Once she declared herself as a Jane her vague interest in art became a true avocation. Let others delve deeply into the cold minds of machines, let others unravel the secrets of the double helix; she would learn the timeless truths to be found in art. It was a perfectly useless thing to learn, according to her mother. It would never earn her a dime, never get her a place in a competitive university. It would never make her rich.

And yet, now, as Miss Violet Blake gazed out over the landscape below the shuttle, she alone understood what it represented.

The young man named Mo'Steel was descending, hand over hand, one powerful leg wrapped around the thin cable. He landed on the back wall of the shuttle's cargo bay. Then, still holding the wire, he tightrope-walked out along the declining edge of the tail and finally hopped to the ground.

He stood almost directly on the impossible dividing line between the gray canyon and the brilliant meadow.

The canyon was unmistakable to Violet. It was an Ansel Adams. A photograph, not a painting.

The meadow, with the frenetic river cutting through it, was more difficult. Not a Cézanne, the colors were too bold. Van Gogh? Perhaps. Monet? Yes, possibly. But, if she'd had to pick one answer on a multiple-choice test she'd have said Bonnard. Pierre Bonnard.

Mo'Steel was kicking his way through impossible plants that seemed to have been assembled out of swatches of lavender and emerald, apricot and gold.

"Careful, Miss Blake, don't lean out too far," Jobs said. He was at her elbow.

Violet drew back. "I suppose you're right." She glanced over her shoulder. She kept expecting her mother to come striding up, ready to take charge and begin rapping out orders. But Wylson Lefkowitz-Blake was only in the earliest stages of revival. Two others had assumed complete consciousness, their awakening perhaps accelerated by the horrific event that had resulted in the doctor's death. In any case, all three had been in berths close to that tragedy.

Mo'Steel walked a little distance out into the colorful meadow. He looked up and waved, his face a broad, slightly deranged grin. "Come on down. It is deeply weird down here."

The girl 2Face yelled down, "Okay, Mo, stay close, okay?" Then, in an aside to Jobs and Errol, said, "Weird doesn't begin to describe it. One or the other, maybe, but two totally different environments divided so sharply?"

It occurred to Violet that there was irony here. 2Face, a girl whose own face encompassed two entirely opposed concepts, the lovely and the hideous, found this bifurcation disturbing.

"It has to be artificial," Errol said, not for the first time. "You'd almost think it was man-made."

"If I may . . ." Violet Blake began.

Olga Gonzalez came up the stairs and announced, "We found some water!"

She carried a translucent plastic gallon jug, three-quarters full. "We were able to bleed it off the hibernation machinery." She was in one of her more manic moods. Violet had seen these moods turn to despair within a moment's time.

"You think it's safe to drink?" 2Face asked.

Olga shrugged. "We have the equipment from the storage lockers. The chemical testing strips are all long gone, of course. But the microscope still works and at least I don't see any obvious microorganisms. It's as clean as distilled water. Which is not to say there aren't other contaminants. I gave it a taste. No alkali taste. Nothing obvious. I won't bore you with a list of colorless, tasteless, odorless pathogens that might be present in fatal concentrations."

2Face took the bottle and raised it to her lips. She had to use a finger to keep the liquid from dribbling out the disfigured side of her mouth.

She handed the jug to Errol. The water made its rounds, everyone desperately thirsty. Only Yago drank too deeply, swallowing more than his share.

"Maybe that water in the river is drinkable," Shy Hwang suggested. "And there may be edible fruit around."

"If I may . . ." Violet began again.

"None of the food on board survived," Olga said. "Not in any edible form, anyway. There's some powdery residue in some of the freeze-dried packs, but I doubt there's any nutritive value."

"Great, so we starve?" Yago said.

"Let's get down to the ground, then we can see what's what," Jobs said. "Who's next?"

"I'll stay," Errol said. "So we can see about belaying this cable in such a way as we can use it to run a bosun's chair up and down to ferry the weak and the wounded." He glanced at Billy Weir, who had been propped into a sitting position. His undead eyes stared out across the landscape below.

"And the dead folks," Jobs said. "Sooner or later I guess we'll have to get all these people down and bury them." Jobs continued, "I'll stay here with you, Errol. I can work on the bosun's chair. We have some tools now, from the chest. I can strip panels from the bulkheads and make a frame from decking."

He actually seemed mildly excited by the project. *A true techie,* Violet thought with distaste. *One of those people.*

"I wish I knew what was down there," Shy Hwang said. "It's so . . . there could be anything. Wild animals, deadly snakes, things we haven't even thought of."

"If I may . . ." Violet said a third time.

"What? You want to say something, Jane?" 2Face snapped at her.

"If I may, I was going to offer some reassurance. I doubt you'd find wild beasts in early-twentieth-century France."

2Face stared at her. "Uh-huh. Well, thanks for the update on France." She shot a look to Jobs, a look suggesting the possibility that Violet was crazy, possibly dangerously so.

"I believe this landscape was derived from a painting. Monet or Bonnard, I think."

"What are you talking about?" Olga demanded.

"The gray-shade is derived from an Ansel Adams photograph. Or at least from someone mimicking Adams's style. The detail can only be photographic. But this sky, this meadow, that river are all clearly derived from a painting. Pierre Bonnard was a —"

"She's right!" Yago cried. "It's a painting. It's not even real. We've been worrying about a painting."

"Mo's walking around down there," Jobs pointed out. "It's not flat. It's not a painting."

"I suggested it was derived from a painting, not that it *is* a painting," Miss Blake said patiently. "I think it's likely that whoever created this place used an Adams photo and an Impressionist painting to . . . to imagine . . . these environments."

"Who are you talking about?" Shy Hwang asked.

Violet was feeling a bit put out. They were staring at her accusingly. She was flustered and couldn't think of a ready answer.

"Aliens?" Jobs whispered.

"Well, *someone*," Miss Blake said. "Surely you see that this meadow and this gray-shade canyon, not to mention that sky, did not occur naturally."

"Aliens," Jobs said more confidently now. "That's how the ship came to be standing upright. That's what happened. We didn't land. We were captured."

"Captured by art lovers?" 2Face demanded, incredulous.

"Most likely that this was done for our benefit," Violet suggested. "Perhaps the aliens are merely trying to be polite."

Jobs said, "We found a rack of DD's — data disks — in the lockers, along with the tools and the decayed food."

"Presumably an effort on NASA's part to keep alive some portion of the human cultural legacy," Shy Hwang suggested.

"Including art?" 2Face wondered. "Fine, but you're saying someone created this environment for us? Using the DD's? How? The data was in the locker. It wasn't loaded into any accessible system."

"They were on the ship," Jobs said. "Whoever did all this, whoever created this environment? They had to have been aboard this ship."

(CHAPTER TEN)

"THE BABY . . . SOMETHING'S NOT RIGHT."

Jobs was one of the last to set foot on the planet's surface. He had stayed behind to fashion a bosun's chair that was used to ferry some of the less-agile Wakers, as they were now called. Now he was ready to go down himself.

He was reluctant. It wasn't that the surface frightened him — it fascinated him. The poet within him found it stirring. But the poet was a subset, a mere file within the hard-core techie. This ship was Earth. This ship was human technology. He could unscrew panels and look inside and understand what he was seeing. He could follow fiber-optic pathways and know why they went where they went.

It was like a museum, of course. The shuttle and the *Mayflower* capsule within it were a strange mixture of cutting-edge toys and antique systems. Old and new.

Somehow, it had actually worked. It had carried them for five centuries and more through space. Jobs felt intense admiration for that, for what it represented in terms of human ingenuity.

Their numbers had grown. Jobs's little brother, Edward, had awakened, and by a stroke of luck Jobs had been able to keep him from seeing their parents. Or what was left of them.

Miss Blake's mother was awake now, as well as three other kids, a ten-year-old who called himself Roger Dodger, a fourteen-year-old girl named Tate, and a sixteen-year-old guy named Anamull.

And D-Caf had awakened.

That made seventeen people in all. Seventeen thirsty, hungry people.

Emotional breakdowns were common. Grief was a virus that spread from one to another, was suppressed only to mutate, take on some new aspect, and attack again.

Jobs and Errol had worked out a pulley system to allow them to reascend to the *Mayflower*. That way people could serve watches aboard, waiting for others to revive.

But now it was time, at last, for Jobs to leave the ship.

Jobs slid down the main cable. He would have liked to use the bosun's chair, but he was unwilling to look like one of the lame. Not with Mo'Steel grinning up at him.

"So. What do you think, Duck?" Mo'Steel asked, indicating the landscape.

Down at ground level the weirdness of it was infinitely more pronounced. Jobs straddled the line between environments. One foot was planted in gray dust. The other crunched thick, irregular grass.

To the left a vast canyon yawned, impossibly deep, impossibly steep. Silent, immeasurably huge. Perfectly detailed until you looked too closely, and then you could see quite clearly that the dust was not dust but identical round pebbles. And everything, the rocks, the few gray cacti, were all made up of those same gray-shade pebbles.

"Pixels," Jobs said. "The original photo was predigital. This is the max resolution, I guess."

Mo'Steel nodded sagely. "Watch this." He picked up a small rock and threw it as far out into the canyon as he could.

"Uh-huh," Jobs said.

"Shh. Listen. You hear that?"

Jobs heard the rock hit bottom. It had hit bottom long before it should have.

Together they walked into the gray world. They stood at the edge of the canyon and looked down. Impossible not to believe it was real. You could feel the depth of the canyon in your soul. But when Jobs threw a second rock after the first it, too, fell for no more than five seconds before landing with a tiny rattling sound.

"Know what else? Look up at the sky. Look at that cloud up there."

Jobs obeyed. He saw a puffy white, lavender-edged cloud moving serenely toward the border between environments. It reached the edge of the gray-shade environment and kept blowing. As it crossed the line it lost all color, gained clarity, and was absorbed into the sky above the canyon.

Mo'Steel seemed to expect him to say something penetrating, but all he could manage was, "Huh."

Jobs walked back into the world of color, bent down, and stroked a single shaft of grass. Of course it was not grass. It was three inches across, a quarter-inch thick, smeared with green and blue.

He pulled at it and it came free. He stared at the root structure with Mo'Steel leaning over his shoulder.

"Look at that, Mo. The root structure looks normal. The dirt looks normal. Not like the dirt over in the canyon. This is like actual dirt. The roots are like actual roots. The leaf, though, no way."

"Tastes like grass," Mo'Steel said.

"You tried to eat it?"

Mo'Steel shrugged. "Hey, we gotta eat, right? I thought maybe you could eat it. But it's like eating what the lawn mower left behind."

Jobs sighed. He looked at the lost, confused, wondering, grieving gaggle of humans, all together in the Impressionist environment. They looked shabby and dull in this vivid landscape. Hard-edged, definite, almost vulgar in their detail. His brother was staring up at a sketchy tree.

"What are we going to do?" Jobs wondered.

Mo'Steel shook his head. "I was hoping you'd know."

"I am lost," Jobs said. He took a deep breath. "No food. No water. Not much, anyway. Whoever put this all together, aliens or whatever, they got the air right. They got the roots of these plants right. But I doubt there's real water in that river over there."

"Let's go see."

But Jobs was too distracted to answer. "They're playing mix and match, that's the problem."

"Who is?"

"Them. The aliens. They don't have a context. They downloaded our data, but they don't know what's real and what isn't, what's actual and what's just, you know, art or imagination. See, they found technical data on air quality so we have air. Or maybe it's just the natural air of this planet. Maybe they have scientific descriptions of plants, so they got the roots right, but they don't know what to do about the pictures and stuff."

Mo'Steel said, "Hey, there must have been stuff about us, right? About humans? Like what we are, what we need to eat and drink and all?"

"I don't know, Mo. You look in an encyclopedia under 'humans' you don't exactly find a guide for the care and feeding of same. Probably says we're omnivorous. If they access a dictionary they can figure out that means we eat anything. That may not be a good thing, depending on how these aliens interpret it."

Jobs looked up at the shuttle. It was stupendously out of place. The white-painted shuttle was pockmarked with a thousand micrometeorite holes. The solar sails hung limp and crumpled, like carelessly hung laundry or broken arms. The Mylar sheen was gone, the microsheeting was dull.

Jobs and Mo'Steel had gone extra-vehicular to

deploy those sails. Hanging there in orbit around Earth they'd seen the Rock slam into it. They'd seen the planet ripped apart, shattered into three big, mismatched, irregular chunks.

Yesterday in Jobs's mind and memory. It had happened yesterday.

Jobs's parents were up there in the *Mayflower*. Dead. Yesterday he'd seen them alive, yesterday they had walked aboard the shuttle with him and settled into those berths beside him. But that was five-hundred years ago. When had they died? Had it happened right away? Or had they survived for centuries, only to die at the last minute?

There came a sound of raised voices from the dozen Wakers. An argument. Yago's voice was heard most clearly.

Jobs and Mo'Steel joined the group.

"What's the beef?" Jobs asked Errol in a whisper.

He and Errol had formed a working relationship based on mutual respect. Errol was an actual rocket scientist, a fuel systems designer. An engineer. He had come aboard the *Mayflower* with his wife and their one child, a girl. The girl's berth had been perforated by a micrometeorite. It had drilled a hole right through her heart. His wife was cheese.

It was something else Jobs shared with Errol: a

need to keep busy in order to hold the avalanche of grief at bay.

"It's the sergeant and her . . . her baby," Errol said. "The baby . . . something's not right."

The baby was still in its mother's arms. Not crying. But looking around with its empty eyes as though searching for something. And the more its searched, the more agitated its mother became.

"Something is going to happen," Tamara Hoyle muttered. "Something is happening right now."

(CHAPTER ELEVEN)

"YOU MAY NEED A SOLDIER."

"It's some kind of a freak — if it's even human!" Yago cried. "Look at it! Look at the two of them. Am I the only one seeing this?"

2Face was already sick of Yago. He was a pampered monster, a spoiled brat with DNA-manipulated good looks and an awesome level of selfishness.

But he was right about the baby. There was something wrong.

The baby turned its head to look left. Tamara Hoyle turned her head to the left.

Puppet master and puppet? Or just some exaggeration of the natural sympathy between mother and child?

The baby stared right at Yago and Tamara's eyes drilled into him. Identical expressions of fixed focus.

"Look! Look at that! Don't you people see? They're connected!" Yago yelled.

Olga said, "The umbilical cord's — if that's what it was — has been cut."

"Cut?" Yago shrilled. "And do you see a difference? You want to know the difference? The difference is the doctor is dead." He stabbed an accusing finger at Tamara and her baby. "She's a killer. A killer and a freak."

"What is it you want?" 2Face calmly asked Yago.

"A little order, that's all," Yago said. "We need some rules here. And we need those rules right from the start. Rule number one in any society is: You don't let murderers go free."

"We don't have a judge or a courtroom," 2Face pointed out. They'd been over this. And they had other, more pressing problems. "We don't have any way to lock her up. And we need her to care for her baby. Are you going to do it?"

"We don't need a court. Eye for an eye," Yago hissed. "She's a freak. A murdering freak. She should be driven out. Exiled. You let her and that freak alien baby stay, you'll regret it."

"All right, no one is exiling anyone," 2Face snapped. This was hitting close to home. If the baby was a freak, so, maybe, was 2Face. "We're all that's left of the human race; we're not going to start drawing lines and saying who's in and who's out."

"I see," Yago said. "And you'll take responsibility if this woman and her so-called baby create more trouble?"

2Face swallowed, hesitated. She'd seen Yago's trap too late. He was putting her together with Tamara and the baby. He was making her responsible for whatever they did. "Yes," she said at last.

"We won't forget you said that," Yago said. "And anyway, I suspect most people here don't agree with you. How about you, Ms. Lefkowitz-Blake? What do you think? I know my mother always admired your judgment."

Wylson Lefkowitz-Blake blinked, surprised and flattered, but quickly seized the tendered opportunity. "I think it's too soon to foreclose any options. Let's get the facts first, then we can reach a reasoned judgment."

Yago let 2Face see his triumph, his sneering "gotcha" look.

Tamara Hoyle seemed to ignore the drama entirely. "Something is coming," she whispered. She and her baby stared toward the distant river. The baby smiled.

2Face knew she'd been outmaneuvered. She'd known to expect it, known that Yago would make a move sooner or later. He was a bully, but not a simple one. He was, after all, the president's son, someone raised in the political life.

She told herself it didn't matter because now that more adults were awake her tenuous, accidental authority would have been displaced anyway. But she resented that Yago had engineered it. He had acted as the kingmaker. Or queenmaker, in this case.

It had happened in a heartbeat. Yago had neatly pulled the rug out from under her.

Within ten minutes after Yago's move Wylson Lefkowitz-Blake, the Jane's mother, was confidently pushing people around, bringing order out of chaos, detailing a search party, setting watches for duty back aboard the ship, organizing the unpacking of the shuttle's tools and instruments.

Fine, 2Face told herself. *Truth was, the woman was better qualified to be in charge; she was the founder of a multibillion-dollar empire, of course she was in charge.*

That wasn't the problem. The problem was that 2Face didn't like being outmaneuvered by Yago. And she didn't want to be made responsible for the actions of the Marine sergeant and her eerie child.

Yago was right: There was something wrong

there. But not only there. There was something wrong with Billy Weir as well. 2Face couldn't put her finger on it, but Billy made the hair stand up on the back of her neck. He was alive, his pupils reacted to light, but he'd said nothing, moved no muscle. They'd given him water and he'd swallowed some of it, that had been his greatest accomplishment so far.

2Face was as hungry and thirsty as anyone, as disturbed by the impossible landscape of this alien world. But she'd taken comfort in the distraction of being in charge. Now she was "one of the kids" in a world where the adults were reasserting them-selves, especially Wylson Lefkowitz-Blake.

With less to do, there was more time to think. She didn't want to think.

Wylson wasted no time getting rid of her.

"Okay, Mr. Hwang, you take your daughter and this one" — Wylson pointed at Mo'Steel — "over to take a look at the river. Come back and let us know if it's actual water. Carry some jugs with you, might as well not waste a trip."

"Send me, too," Tamara Hoyle said.

"I don't think we're going to be using you," Wyl-son said, making no attempt to disguise her con-tempt.

"I'm a trained soldier," Tamara argued. "You may need a soldier."

"You're a murderer with a freak baby," Yago said. He had attached himself to Wylson.

Tamara's baby turned away, and a moment later, so did Tamara, as though the issue no longer interested either of them.

"Okay, you'd better get going," Wylson said to Shy Hwang.

Shy Hwang nodded to his daughter and Mo'-Steel. He looked a little sheepish, but determined. 2Face saw he was ready to reassert his prerogatives as her father. That was good, actually. 2Face loved her father. He had a right to be a father.

They picked up a couple of empty gallon jugs and set off through the brilliant cornhusk "grass."

Mo'Steel forged ahead, the only one of the three who was remotely excited by the adventure.

Let it go, 2Face told herself. She touched her face, quite unconsciously, as she recalled the price that could be paid by the vengeance-seeker.

CHAPTER TWELVE

"THEY'RE HEADING FOR OUR PEOPLE!"

"It was peaceful," Shy Hwang said to his daughter.

It took her a moment to track. Was he talking about Yago's coup? The disturbing landscape?

No, of course not. He meant her mom's death. 2Face blushed with the good half of her face.

"I know, Dad. We were all asleep. She was asleep. It was peaceful."

Her father let out a stifled sob. He wiped tears from his eyes and set his face in a parody of determination.

2Face had never thought much about her parents' relationship. It had always been there. They argued occasionally but made up quickly. But of course they'd been together for seven years before 2Face was born. Not that 2Face wasn't devastated by her mother's death. But, to her shame, she had to admit that her father's grief was deeper, more personal.

She resisted the insidious edge of contempt for her father. It was right that he grieve. She was the bad one, she was the one who was failing her mother's memory. Her father was reacting the way a man who loved his wife should.

And yet, he had to be able to see that there was a crisis before them, a mess that required action.

He'd be okay. He'd be okay in time. That was it, he needed time.

Why didn't she? How had she turned so quickly away from grief? Maybe she was more resilient. Or maybe she was just more cold-blooded, less feeling than her father.

She reached for her father to take his arm, to comfort him, but something held her back. Instead she said, "Maybe we should hurry up or Mo will get way ahead of us."

Shy Hwang shook his head, trying again to resume the mantle of parental authority. "No. I'll call him back. We should stick together and take our time. We're in a strange place."

He yelled to Mo'Steel, who pretended not to understand his words and simply waved back.

So 2Face and her father accelerated their pace, passing beneath a sketchy tree whose trunk seemed to have been constructed of three or four irregular slices of bark piled together.

Brush strokes. Miss Blake might be a simpering throwback, but she was right about this. It was all some weird 3-D representation of a painting. How had they done it, the aliens? Holograms and force fields? Genetic manipulation? Or was none of this real and the Wakers were still sleeping, sharing the same dream?

One thing was for sure: If any of this was real, the aliens, if aliens they were, had vast powers. It had to require enormous energies to excavate the gray-shade canyon, enormous power to grow this fabulously strange landscape.

Why? Why would an alien race want to do this? What was the motive — there had to be one. At least it wasn't an aggressive move, that much was obvious. The aliens had gone to a lot of trouble to create an environment for their human guests. That had to be good news. In fact, very good news.

No, 2Face told herself, *the real dangers were from within, from Yago and Billy Weir and Tamara and the baby.*

Mo'Steel had reached the river and was waving

them forward enthusiastically. They pushed on through the clinging pseudo-grass. At least it was downhill now.

The river was like the trees, a jumble of agitated, moving, tumbling brush strokes. Up close you could see that it wasn't liquid at all, not in the way it behaved, not in the way it moved. It reminded 2Face of watching clothes in the dryer, tumbling, roiling bits of blue and green and flecks of white in motion.

"It's not water," Shy Hwang said, disappointed.

But Mo'Steel grinned. "Watch this." He knelt down and pushed his plastic pitcher into what seemed so solid. The brush stroke of blue came apart, sprayed around the obstacle, and to 2Face's amazement, water, actual clear water began to fill the jug.

"Is that water?" 2Face asked.

Mo'Steel tipped the jug up to his mouth and drank. "It's not Pepsi," he said and passed the jug to 2Face.

It was water. Or something that sure tasted and felt like water, though unpleasantly lukewarm.

"Water," Shy Hwang agreed.

"Hey," Mo'Steel said. He was frowning, staring off into the distance. "Hey, scope that."

The creatures were on the far side of the river

and about a thousand feet upstream. They were moving, standing it seemed, but moving swiftly, effortlessly. Almost as if they were riding horses that were obscured by the grass.

They were the color of rust or dried blood. It was impossible to gauge their size. From a distance they appeared to be no more than man-sized, but with a multiplicity of spidery legs and very possibly more than one head.

They were surely not anything envisioned by Miss Blake's Pierre Bonnard, the artist who had painted this meadow and this river.

They veered suddenly and zoomed effortlessly across the water.

"They're heading for our people!" 2Face said. "Come on!"

They started running. Running and yelling. There was no sign that the others had spotted the alien Riders.

"Hey! Hey!" Mo'Steel yelled. "Look! Look!"

But it was too far for voices to carry clearly. It looked as if the main group was huddled in some sort of debate.

The Riders moved swiftly, faster than a running human, not so fast as a car. They were three points of a collapsing triangle: 2Face and her group, the main group of Wakers, and the Riders. The Riders would reach the Wakers first.

Then, the Wakers noticed. 2Face thought she saw Tamara pointing. There was a faint sound of yelling.

2Face was gasping, panting, as out of shape as . . . as a person who'd been asleep for five-hundred years. Mo'Steel had farther to run but he'd caught up with 2Face and Shy Hwang and was now pulling ahead.

2Face saw the Wakers drawing closer together, instinctively gathering their strength. The Riders — there seemed to be half a dozen — slowed and stopped twenty or thirty feet from Wylson Lefkowitz-Blake, who stepped out front, hands held out, palms up.

2Face saw Wylson shake her head. Then again, more violently. One of the Riders was on the move, zooming back and forth in front of her, seeming to taunt her, waving a curved stick like a dull-bladed scimitar at her.

It was a challenge. A challenge to battle.

Wylson shook her head adamantly and Errol moved forward, the gallant, seeking to put himself between Wylson and the gaunt Rider.

The Rider tossed the curved stick at Errol and Errol snatched it out of the air. He looked at it, seemed to be trying to figure out what it was or how to hold it.

There was a horrific shriek, an unearthly cry that was like metal gears grinding on ball bearings.

The Rider zoomed forward and stabbed a spear into Errol's thigh. Errol fell to one knee.

Mo'Steel was almost there. He was going to charge the Rider but two other Riders swooped in to block him. 2Face could see now what they rode. Not animals, but nearly flat, circular disks less than four feet in diameter. There was no obvious engine. No way for the Riders even to hold on but by careful balance. They seemed to steer with their weight, leaning this way or that. The disks would scoot, with gathering speed, just inches above the grass tops.

The two outriders blocked Mo'Steel and he came to a confused stop. 2Face caught up with him, grabbed his arm to keep him from doing anything stupid.

Up close now, 2Face's impression was confirmed: The creatures had two distinct, but different heads. At least one of them did. The other Rider had a stump, six inches of neck and nothing on top.

They stood on two jointed legs, each split into two short calves or elongated feet. The legs were jointed at the hip, at the split, again halfway down the calves, then at what might be ankles. The upper body was narrow and rigid, almost glossy, like a beetle's carapace. They had two long arms, jointed much like human arms, and four-fingered hands.

The heads were the only break with symmetry. One head was little more than a mouth stuck on a neck, a hideous, razor-toothed sock-puppet of a head.

The other, what had to be the main head, was dominated by two large, glittery gold compound eyes, like a fly's but with fewer facets. Directly below, a row of four smaller eyes, black irises in gold orbs. The mouth was small, round, and seemed to be the origin of that terrible metallic voice.

The lead Rider, or surfer as he now seemed, zoomed a circle around Errol, taunting him in his harsh voice, jabbing a hand at the weapon in Errol's hand.

Errol used the weapon as a crutch, stood hobbling on one leg. Then, far too slowly, with no possible way to fool his antagonist, Errol swung the scimitar, caught nothing but air, and was carried over by his momentum. He fell facedown on hands and knees. The alien stabbed him in his back and Errol cried out.

Again the taunting, the circling.

"Stop it! Stop it!" 2Face screamed, and realized

she was not the only one. Almost everyone was yelling or crying, but no one could move as the gliding Riders formed a sort of moving circle around the two combatants.

Errol was panting, sobbing, facedown in the brilliant grass. He made a feeble attempt to stand up. That movement was all the alien needed. He swept in, stabbed his spear into the back of Errol's neck, and twisted it savagely. Errol was no more.

The aliens rode away a few paces, stopped, grouped together. 2Face had reached the others. Everyone stood, waiting, helpless. Mo'Steel started for Errol's dropped scimitar.

"No!" Jobs yelled. "Mo! Don't do it. Don't touch it! It's a challenge, let it lie, let it lie."

Mo'Steel hesitated, fingers just inches from the hilt. The aliens watched him.

Slowly Mo'Steel took a step back. "Not this time," he said to the killer. "Later on. We'll see."

The aliens took a last look, turned, and sped away out of sight.

CHAPTER THIRTEEN

"YOU DON'T GO DEER HUNTING WITH A TANK."

Night came to the meadow, a night of strange amethyst clouds and orange swirls in a troubled sky.

Violet Blake found it fascinating. Was this scene an actual painting? Or were the aliens riffing on a theme? It might be Bonnard, or not. Was whoever or whatever operated the machinery on this strange world now composing its own art?

No one else seemed to care. They'd managed to make a small fire of the improbable grass and even more improbable wood. They were beside the river now, and so everyone had water to drink, and even wash in.

The shuttle stood at a distance, unlit except by starlight. It seemed strangely small. Lonely.

Violet's mother was still in charge, as much as anyone could be said to be in charge of the scared, shaken, disorganized rabble. They huddled together talking endlessly, planning, abandoning plans, plotting, squabbling. Violet's mother was trying to hold a board meeting. Trying to transfer the skills she had honed in big business to this situation. Demanding concrete answers from people who had only speculation to offer.

Yago was her toadie, seconding every motion, clinging tightly to what power there was, calling her "boss." He was a work of art himself, Yago was, artificial, at least to some degree. Cat DNA in his petri-dish golden eyes caused them to glow in the dark. Maybe his perfect bronze skin was a natural product of his African-American mother and Caucasian father, but Violet doubted it.

In return for the shameless toadying, Violet's mother favored her one sure ally, complimenting Yago's good sense. They were getting to be quite an act.

Olga Gonzalez, Mo'Steel's mother, had little to say except on matters to do with biology, her scientific speciality. She had a great deal to say about the anomalies in the plant life — the mismatch between what was taking place at the cellular level and what was observable in the developed species. But when Wylson demanded information on the aliens, Olga could only plead ignorance.

"There's no such thing as an expert on alien biology," Olga snapped after repeated questioning. "We've never encountered aliens. You know as much as I do."

Shy Hwang sat cross-legged with head hung down, lost in memory. From time to time he would reach for his daughter, to hold her close, to hug her, and at those times Violet felt a twinge of jealousy and resentment at 2Face's grudging response. 2Face seemed a cold little creature to her.

Another adult Waker had emerged from the shuttle, a man named Daniel Burroway, yet another scientist, an astrophysicist. He was an arrogant man, convinced of his own brilliance, and, it seemed to Violet, almost brutally indifferent to the fact that the three other members of his family had not survived. He talked a lot. If there was anyone who would challenge Wylson, it would be Burroway.

Billy Weir lay silent. Still. Jobs tended to him, paying more attention to him than to his own brother, Edward, who hummed to himself while making little collections of leaves and rocks. Some of the other younger kids sat crying, as alone as kids could be.

The newly awakened sixteen-year-old named Anamull stared, slack-jawed, into the fire. A burnout, Violet guessed. A big, hulking kid with brown hair and steroid arms, and no affect.

D-Caf sat by himself, too, ignored, excluded, shunned. According to Jobs, D-Caf had fired the shot that killed the mission's copilot. A killer, though he seemed more pathetic than dangerous to Violet. He kept smiling at people, looking for an acceptance that no one would offer. He was jumpy, energetic, a shaggy puppy who couldn't understand why he'd been spanked and put in the corner.

It was not a group to inspire confidence, Violet thought.

And then there was Tamara Hoyle. Along with her own mother, the type of woman Violet disliked most. A mannish woman. When she stood it was at parade rest, when she sat it was with legs precisely folded and back perfectly straight. She looked as if, all other things being equal, she could fight any of the men and win.

But all other things were not equal. Tamara Hoyle held the eyeless baby that never ate, never cried, only chuckled from time to time, as if at some secret joke. The baby was a cherub with a knowing, leering, too-wise face.

The mother might almost have seemed indifferent to the child. She never looked at her baby. She never comforted it. She carried it easily, place to place, always holding it face-out as if she were allow-ing it to see the world. Of course the baby could not possibly see.

"They can't be the ones who created all of this," Daniel Burroway was arguing in his loud and pedantic tone. "These aliens you describe, Riders or surfers, whatever appellation you choose, were clearly warriors of some sort. It requires a subtler intelligence to imagine this environment, to meld the biologically functional with the artistic. As Dr. Gonzalez has confirmed, these are, biologically speaking, common plants. The grass is grass, despite the overt physical differences. That all argues for a larger intelligence than the sort of brutes you describe."

Violet Blake could dispute that point — many violent societies had created great art and shown great intellectual creativity. But she didn't have the will or the energy to be argumentative at the moment. She was desperately tired and hungry. The talk was going nowhere, accomplishing nothing.

If her opinion was asked for she would give it. But anything she said would almost surely lead to a clash with her mother and her sycophant, Yago.

Jobs evidently felt no such hesitation. "I agree with Dr. Burroway, but not for his reasons."

Burroway frowned. "Then please, do tell," he said with a mock bow.

"It's that any warrior society uses its cutting-edge technology for fighting. I mean, humans, right? The military had planes before civilians, used rockets before civilians did, set up the Internet, global positioning, nuclear power plants, lasers, on and on. Now, those surfboards the Riders are using, it is cool technology, no question, but it's not the cutting edge for whoever did all this terra forming. Or art forming, whatever you call it. I'm just saying, anyone who can split the sky right down the middle into a gray sky and a blue sky, or cause water to flow in packets . . . they can do better than antigravity skateboards, or whatever those things were. Not to mention spears and swords."

Violet was amused to hear such a ready flow of words. Jobs was not a great talker, unless the subject was technology.

"The Riders might be the aliens' pets, for all we know," 2Face said. "Or maybe . . ." She paused, sending a direct question to Violet. "Maybe those Riders are part of the scene. I mean, maybe they're images drawn from the same data the aliens took this environment. Is that possible?"

Violet heard her mother snort dismissively. "I think maybe we should stick to talking about ways to deal with the situation. This is not an art seminar."

"Could be those Riders just didn't think it was woolly enough using ray guns or whatever," Mo'-Steel suggested, speaking for the first time. "Maybe they weren't looking for a gimme. Maybe they were looking to squeeze the A gland."

Pretty much everyone stared at him, mystified.

Jobs translated. "He's saying maybe I'm wrong. Maybe the Riders do have better technology but this isn't them making war against us, this is just them, you know, engaging in a sport. Maybe they were looking for a challenge, a thrill. Squeeze the A gland — you know, adrenal gland."

"You don't go deer hunting with a tank," Anamull agreed.

Violet hadn't thought he was even listening.

Then, "What's that?" D-Caf cried and leaped to his feet. "Shh! I heard something."

Silence.

The sound of something moving through the grass. And then, "Hello? Is anyone there?"

Two people staggered into the firelight. One, a big man, was leaning for support on a smaller man. Violet could see that the larger man's right leg was unable to bear any weight.

The big man dropped to the ground and panted, unable to speak. Then he noticed Billy Weir and uttered a gasp or a sob. He crawled over to him. "Billy! Billy! It's Dad!"

No answer. Billy Weir just stared.

The smaller man said, "Glad to see all of you. I'm very, very glad to see all of you. We saw all the empty berths, we knew others had awakened before us. But we couldn't figure out where you were. Then we saw the fire."

Violet noticed a distinct accent, a sort of lilt. The man was dark-skinned but with Caucasian features. Indian, Violet guessed.

Olga stood up and carried a water jug to the injured man, then offered it to the other newcomer.

"My name's Tathagata Rajagopalachari. I am afraid that my American friends call me T.R. My companion there is William Weir. He said to call him Big Bill. He is hurt, as you can see."

"Welcome to both of you," Wylson said. "What do you do, T.R.?"

"Do? Oh, yes. I am a psychiatrist."

Violet almost laughed at the silent consternation that announcement caused.

The other man moaned in pain and grabbed his leg hard, as though trying to squeeze the pain out of it. He paid no attention to the group but kept up his effort to get a response from his son.

"Do you have a doctor?" T.R. asked. "As I said, my friend here is not well. And I am afraid that my medical training occurred a very long time ago indeed."

"You're the closest thing we have to a doctor," Olga said. "I'm a biologist but I don't have an M.D., not even one from a long time ago."

T.R. nodded. "Oh, that is distressing. Perhaps among the other survivors?"

Wylson shook her head. "So far we're it, Doctor. We expect a few more Wakers like the two of you, but as you saw, the rest did not survive the trip."

T.R. frowned. "As I saw? But I saw nothing to suggest any such thing."

"We're talking about the variously decomposed corpses in the berths," Burroway said impatiently.

"But . . . But I looked carefully. I observed five more individuals in states of rest, two of them beginning to awaken, but there were no dead. The other berths were empty."

CHAPTER FOURTEEN

"AND MAYBE WE'RE ANTS TRYING TO FIGURE OUT A PICNIC."

Jobs descended the circular stairway slowly, cautiously, on guard despite the fact that Mo'Steel was already halfway down the length of the *Mayflower* capsule.

The berths where Jobs's parents had been were empty. Not only empty, clean. No trace of the hideous mold. No fragments of decayed clothing.

Level after level, empty berths that had once been coffins. All of them gone but five. Three in deep slumber, two more, as T.R. had said, were waking.

It was hard to accept. The horrific images were permanently copied onto Jobs's brain. The ones who had been cratered, the cheesers, the facelifts, the wormers. All gone.

Jobs and Mo'Steel went to the two newly

emerging Wakers. They were groggy, confused, scared. Jobs filled them in on the basic facts: the vertical landing, the artwork landscape, the five-hundred years, the deaths. He left out the vicious aliens, the freakish baby, the silent Billy Weir, the deaths of Doctor Huerta and Errol.

Plenty of time for that later.

Of the two Wakers, one was a kid, one an adult. They were father and son. The father was Alberto DiSalvo, an engineer who had worked on the solar sails. His son, age fifteen, called himself Kubrick.

Jobs motioned Mo'Steel to follow him out of hearing of the new Wakers who, in any event, seemed to be falling back to sleep in the familiar pattern.

"How many does that make?" Jobs asked Mo'-Steel.

"Twenty-three Wakers. Minus the doctor and old Errol. Twenty-one up and running."

"Three more still on ice," Jobs said. "Where'd the others go?"

"The dead ones?"

"Uh-uh. Twenty-one awake, plus the doctor and Errol, plus three asleep, right? Twenty-six? We counted thirty-four we thought were alive. That leaves eight people gone who we thought were alive who aren't here or back outside."

Olga was up above them, watching from the entryway. She leaned over to call down the stairwell. "You kids okay in there?"

"Yeah, Mom," Mo'Steel yelled. "Got two more live ones coming around."

"Eight live ones gone," Jobs muttered. "What's going on here? The Deaders are all vacuumed out and so are eight live ones, but five are left behind, undisturbed. Seven left behind, actually, because it was T.R. who told us the dead were gone. So at that point we had seven people on board. The aliens — or whoever — take the dead and eight live ones. Why?"

Mo'Steel shrugged. "You got me, Duck."

"This is unnecessarily weird," Jobs muttered. "I'm not getting a picture. Maybe my brain is still fuzzy."

"Maybe reality is fuzzy," Mo'Steel said.

"Some aliens bring us neatly down for an easy landing. They invent this bizarre landscape. They or some other bunch come by and kill Errol. Then the Riders or the first aliens or some totally new bunch of aliens, or some combination of them, carry off all the bodies plus probably eight people still coming out of hibernation. And leave seven behind. What's the game?"

"Maybe games. Plural."

"Yeah. And maybe we're ants trying to figure out

a picnic. Wait a minute. When did they do it? When none of us was looking this way? When the Riders attacked?"

"Or else any time since we hauled butt for the river and it got dark."

"Still, the Riders could have been a diversion."

"Yeah. Kind of a mystery, huh?" Mo'Steel said. "Kind of thing you like to climb all over. You love to try and figure out stuff."

Jobs smiled. His friend was not subtle. "You can stop worrying about me, Mo. I'm not going to go nuts or whatever."

"That's good. What are we going to do?"

"You and me, or all of us?"

Mo'Steel shrugged. "Big picture. I mean, it's like we have problems inside and out. Aliens and all, like the ones who killed old Errol. But the serious stuff is like in us, you know? People losing it from sadness. People fighting over who's going to rule. That baby, too."

"Billy Weir," Jobs said.

"Yeah, he's strange but he's not bothering anyone at least."

"I think he's —"

Mo'Steel's mother interrupted, "Kids! Something is happening. Back at the camp."

97

Jobs glanced at the two Wakers. Both dozing still. "Come on."

The three of them were almost back at camp when they saw Big Bill Weir staggering away from the fire. Daniel Burroway, Yago, and Anamull were wielding burning brands. The bright tips drew lurid arcs in the night.

Someone threw a stone or a chunk of wood and hit Bill Weir in the back.

"You've got my son, I have a right!" Big Bill roared.

"Stay at least a hundred yards away," Wylson shouted. "I am deadly serious about that, Mr. Weir."

A burning stick flew, twirling through the air toward Big Bill. Mo'Steel caught the brand and looked to Jobs for guidance.

"What's going on?" Jobs demanded.

"Stay out of it and stay away from him!" Yago snapped. In his other hand he brandished the scimitar the alien Riders had left behind. Jobs had forgotten the weapon. Yago had not.

"They have my son," Big Bill pleaded. He started to say more but his face contorted in pain and choked off his words.

"What is this about?" Olga Gonzalez shouted. "What is going on with you people?"

Yago stepped forward just a few feet, still armed with his torch, and stabbed an accusing finger at the man writhing in pain. "He's got it. You want it, you deal with him."

Daniel Burroway tried to sound reasonable, an impossible task for one red in the face and waving a glowing red branch. "He may be contagious. He's being quarantined. If you come in contact with him you'll be quarantined as well."

Olga was not easily cowed. "Where's the doctor, then?"

"He's a shrink, not a real doctor," Burroway said.

Big Bill moaned and Jobs knelt beside him. "What is it, Mr. Weir?"

"The leg," he gasped.

Jobs hesitated. Maybe they were right. Maybe whatever it was, it was contagious. Or maybe they were just hysterical. Gingerly he lifted the hem of Big Bill's pant leg and tugged at it. The rotten fabric tore easily.

Mo'Steel moved close, bringing the feeble, flickering light of the torch.

Bill Weir's leg was riddled with holes. Tunnels. He looked just like Violet Blake's father and others. A wormer. A live wormer.

Swallowing hard, dreading, not wanting to show

it but unable to conceal his horror, Jobs tore the pant leg some more. The holes were everywhere through the calf muscle, up through the knee. The lower thigh was untouched. But as Jobs stared, he saw a round, red spot of blood appear just above Big Bill's knee. A moment later the spot became a hole and the hole was filled by the pea-green head of a worm.

(CHAPTER FIFTEEN)

"DON'T LET ME LIVE."

Jobs didn't know what to do. Once again his tenuous grip on certainty had been torn away. He'd been engaged in the mystery, trying to understand, and now all that he could see and feel and react to was the foul reality of the killing worm.

He wanted to run away. Should run away. There was no hope for Bill Weir. Was there? Where was Mo? Right there, steady, but grim. Olga? Of course, Mo'Steel's mother stayed by his side.

"It's some kind of worm," Jobs whispered harshly, hoping Big Bill's cries would keep him from overhearing.

"It's nothing I've ever seen or heard of. Not that size, not that fast. Not as a human parasite."

"Can you do anything?" Jobs pleaded.

"I'm not a doctor."

"Mom, it's a bug, right?" Mo'Steel said. "Maybe you could think about how to kill it."

Olga Gonzalez drew her son and Jobs a few paces away. "Look, you need to understand it's very unlikely that this parasite you saw is the only one. That leg may be riddled with them. I have nothing to work with. We have a microscope but we'd need full daylight for that even to work because we don't have a light. No lab. No equipment."

"It's going to eat him alive," Jobs said. "He's conscious. He's not in hibernation like Miss Blake's dad. He's feeling this. And it's only in his leg — it could take a long time for him to die."

"Maybe we cut off his leg," Mo'Steel suggested. "We got Dr. Huerta's scalpel and all."

"That could kill the man," Olga said. "Loss of blood, shock, infection . . . and anyway, it might not stop the parasite. They may have advanced farther than you can see."

"Mom, do we have any other choice?"

Olga looked hard at her son and called him by the name she had given him. "Romeo, this thing could kill all of us. I want to help this man, but you have to understand that the parasite could be capable of infesting anyone in contact. God knows what it is. It may not even be of terrestrial origin. This could be an alien life-form. There's no telling what it might do."

"Oh, oh, help me," Big Bill moaned. "Oh, help me. Oh, help me!" he shrieked, then subsided in sobs.

Jobs said, "Yago has that sword thing the Riders threw to Errol. May be better than a scalpel. Quicker, anyway. In and out fast."

Olga shook her head. "Someone would have to sew up the arteries in his leg or he'd just bleed to death. Someone would have to get in there and do that, with all the risk involved."

"I can do that," a voice said.

Jobs was startled to see Violet Blake. He hadn't noticed her joining them.

"My . . . my dad died from this," Miss Blake said, assuming that clarified her motive.

"You could end up going the same way," Olga said harshly.

"I'll hold him down," Mo'Steel volunteered.

"We don't have any thread," Jobs pointed out. "But we might be able to use optic cable to tie off the arteries."

"Look, this is not the time or the place for self-sacrifice," Olga argued. "That man is probably going to die anyway, no matter what."

"We'll have to get the sword from Yago," Jobs

said. "Ms. Gonzalez, that would be better coming from you. Being an adult. We just need to borrow it. And some more light from the fire."

Olga Gonzalez hesitated. "I can't endanger all of us. I can't endanger my son."

"Hey, danger is my middle name," Mo'Steel said, trying to josh her along.

Jobs could see she was hardening in her opposition. He knew what he felt and what he wanted to say, but putting it into words defeated him. He said, "Ms. Gonzalez, this is . . . We are all that's left of the human race. We have to act like humans. Right?"

"We have to survive," Olga said with finality.

"No, we don't," Violet Blake said. "We don't have to survive, we have to be worthy of survival. I know you're a biologist and maybe you see survival in purely evolutionary terms, but we've evolved beyond being just another bunch of primates, haven't we? Isn't human culture, human morality part of our evolution? Isn't it part of what defines us as a species? If we give that up and start behaving like savages and survive by being savages, have we saved human life or just devolved into some lesser species?"

Jobs stared at her openmouthed. He was struck by intense jealousy, an out-of-place emotion, surely, but undeniable just the same. He'd have given any-thing to be able to speak that way. He noticed Mo'-Steel grinning at him.

"Maybe I should be reading more," Jobs mut-tered under his breath.

Mo'Steel took his mother's hand and held it gen-tly. "Mom, you've never been able to stop me from doing stupid, dangerous stuff that was just about me squeezing the A gland. Now I'm trying to do what's right. Don't stop me now."

"Okay, honey," she said quietly. "Okay. I'll get the sword, or whatever it is."

When she was gone Jobs said, "That was a pretty good speech, Miss Blake."

"Thank you." She knelt beside Big Bill and used the lacy sleeve of her dress to mop sweat from his brow. "We're going to try to help you, Mr. Weir."

The only response was a bellow of pain, a noise so loud that Violet jumped back.

Jobs saw the worm. Or one of the worms, if there were several. It was half out of one hole and digging its way back into untouched flesh. Like a dol-phin going in and out of the waves.

"It's fine to be noble," Jobs said to Mo'Steel, "but if that thing gets me . . . don't let me live."

"Don't think about it, Duck. The Reaper can

smell fear." He laughed and patted Jobs on the back. "You have to put your brain into some other place. Stay happy and the Reaper can't find you."

Despite himself Jobs laughed. "You just make this stuff up to fit the occasion, don't you?"

"Pretty much."

"So you're scared?"

"'Migo, I am seriously scared."

(CHAPTER SIXTEEN)

"I'LL COUNT TO TEN SO YOU'LL KNOW WHEN IT'S HAPPENING."

Jobs heard heated words coming from the main camp. Burroway's loud, grating tone. Wylson Lefkowitz-Blake sounding imperious, but less sure of herself than before. Olga demanding.

In a moment, though, Olga returned carrying the sword. For the first time Jobs looked closely at it. It was curved, almost a scythe. It was perhaps three feet long, very broad, the inside edge was ornate, decorated with cutouts and filigree. There was what might be writing all over the blade. The hilt was never meant for a human hand; it had a clumsy angle in the middle and was too short overall.

"Here's our scalpel," Olga said dryly. "The edge seems quite sharp. I suggest the cut be made about eight inches above the knee. That won't leave him much of a leg, but we have to remove all the affected

portion of the limb. There's no point doing this unless we do it right." She took a deep breath. "I don't
know that I have the strength to handle this thing, or
the eye-hand coordination."

"I can do it," Jobs said.

Olga nodded. "Okay. Romeo? Take Mr. Weir's
shoulders, hold him down, don't let him jerk free. I'll
try to hold his other leg, I'll sit on it, I guess. Miss
Blake, you stand ready with the 'thread.' Jobs, you
know what to do."

When Mo'Steel and his mother were in place,
Violet Blake spoke to Big Bill. "Mr. Weir, we're going
to amputate your leg and try to save you. I'll count
to ten so you'll know when it's happening." She
turned away and mouthed the words *On three* to
Jobs.

He understood. Big Bill would think he had another seven seconds before he needed to panic or
try to break free.

"One . . ." Violet said.

Jobs felt an urgent need to throw up. *Later,* he
told himself. *Throw up later.*

"Two . . ."

Jobs raised the sword.

"Three . . ."

Jobs took careful aim and brought the sword down with all his might.

Jobs breathed.

Mo'Steel stood up and kicked the detached limb away.

Violet Blake moved in to begin suturing the wound. Then she began to scream. She leaped to her feet. She held her right hand out before her, screaming at it.

Jobs saw the worm as it drilled its way down into her index finger. Mo'Steel bounded across the prostrate man and grabbed Violet's wrist. He closed his strong hand around her fingers, leaving only the index finger extended.

"Jobs!" he yelled.

Jobs swung the sword on pure reflex. The blade stopped less than an inch from Mo'Steel's face.

Mo'Steel hauled Violet back and threw her violently into the grass. Jobs yanked Olga to her feet and dragged her away.

Big Bill cried piteously, quietly, "Oh, god, oh, god, it's still here. I can feel it. I can feel it," just before he lost consciousness.

Olga snatched a branch from the fire and blew out the flame leaving only an ember at the tip. She told her son, "Hold her hand. Hold it still," and quickly pressed the coal-hot tip to the stump of Violet Blake's finger.

Violet screamed and fainted, and Jobs missed catching her. She slumped to the ground.

"Back away, back away," Jobs yelled.

They dragged Violet with them, dragged her through the grass and stopped only when they were twenty yards from the hysterical, now-awake Bill Weir.

And then, from the main camp came a new sound, like nothing Jobs had ever heard, a collective moan, a cry of fear and disbelief.

Outlined against the fire a dark form seemed to float through the air. Human? No human moved like that.

And yet with growing dread Jobs realized that he recognized the form, knew what face he would see when at last the shape was close enough.

Billy Weir floated, moved without benefit of muscles, simply floated through the air. He still stared, blank, as though blind, still showed no expression on his vacant face.

He floated with his limbs all limp, with his head upraised, till he was above Big Bill.

Big Bill was shrieking now, shrieking like a lunatic thing, his voice no longer human.

And it seemed to Jobs as though a shadow extended down from Billy Weir to his adoptive father. The shadow enveloped them both. For a heartbeat Big Bill was silent. And then Billy Weir screamed.

Jobs thought at first it was Big Bill again, but no, this voice was different, raw, hoarse, but at least an octave higher, a young voice screaming in pain.

Then silence.

Billy Weir sagged, fell to the ground.

Jobs ran back to him, ran and grabbed his nerveless arms and pulled him away, dragging him back from Big Bill.

He stopped, panting, shaking.

Big Bill was silent. And Jobs knew the man was dead.

(CHAPTER SEVENTEEN)

"TEN'S ONLY A MAGIC NUMBER
IF YOU GOT TEN FINGERS."

"We have to get out of here, right now," Olga said. "Those things could be capable of moving across the ground. Once they're done with Mr. Weir . . ."

Violet Blake heard the words but as if from far away. The pain in her hand was unlike anything she had ever experienced. She would not have believed that a single finger could possibly cause so much agony.

She held her wounded hand with her free hand, using tattered, decaying bits of her dress as a bandage. The blood wouldn't stop. But there was no way to tie a tourniquet, the finger had been lopped off right at the base.

She would have liked to try and sew up whatever vein was producing the endless flow of blood, but she knew she didn't have the nerve for that. The cauterization had been only partly successful.

There was no one to help her. They had dragged the once more prostrate Billy Weir back toward the fire, but they'd been stopped by a solid front presented by Yago, D-Caf, Anamull, Burroway, and the psychiatrist, T.R.

"Wylson says you're quarantined," Yago said. "The worms could be in you."

Violet wanted to scream at him. But the truth was, her mother and the others had been right, the fearful ones, the safe ones, they'd been right and she and her idealistic compatriots had been dangerously wrong. And now even her own mother believed she was contagious.

"The point is we all have to get out of this area," Olga said through gritted teeth.

"Suddenly you discover prudence," Burroway drawled. "A little late, I should say."

Olga erupted. "We're not asking to mingle with you people, we're saying, move. Move! Move now! You want to play gotcha? Do it later."

That seemed to get through. It got through to Violet. She could swear she felt the worms crawling up her legs. She had seen the one in her finger. She had seen it and felt it and known the terror and the pain of it.

Burroway, having gotten off his snide remark,

seemed unsure how to proceed. It was Violet's mother who made the call. "Okay, we move out. We follow the river."

"We should go back to the ship," Jobs said. "There are more Wakers there."

"And maybe more worms," Burroway argued.

"We can't just go off and disappear and leave those people," Jobs argued. "Not to mention the ship. There's a lot of useful things there still. We need tools. We need to make weapons. We need to figure out what happened to all those people who just disappeared. And we have to be there to help the Wakers."

Violet sensed a desperation in Jobs's voice. Of course: He was a techie, leaving the only technology in sight to head out into the wild.

"Forget them," Yago snapped. "Or else you go back, Jobs. You want to be Joe Responsible, you go. But leave the sword with us."

Olga put her hand on Jobs's shoulder. "They're right: We have to get out of this area. We know nothing about these worms. We don't know how they move, how they reproduce. They could be on the ship. They could be all around us soon. We don't know if these are even true parasites: They could be predators. They could hunt us."

Violet let loose a small sob that went unnoticed. There was a battle in her mind between pain and fear, and in that battle fellow-feeling, compassion, concern were all just minor players. She wanted to run away. And more, she wanted to be somewhere else. Back in the world, back on Earth, back in a place where there were doctors and the smell of disinfectant and bright, clean stainless steel gleaming under fluorescent lights.

Suddenly she felt weak. Her knees buckled. She caught herself, terrified of letting any part of her touch the dark ground that in her imagination teemed with the killer worms.

Mo'Steel was at her side in a flash. He caught her around the waist, very chastely, and held her up.

"Strap it up, Miss B., I know it hurts. With pain and all you have to kind of ride right into it. Don't fight it, don't try and look away. You go right straight into the pain. Eat it up, make it yours."

Violet blinked, not understanding the words, but appreciating the tone and the sense that someone was helping her.

Mo'Steel stood close, put his face right into her field of vision. "Don't run from pain. You have to be like, 'Bring it on. Show me what you got.'"

Violet nodded. *Defiance, is that what he meant?* She felt a little stronger and Mo'Steel, evidently sensing this, let her go.

Jobs yelled across the distance to his little brother, telling him to be good and careful and listen to 2Face and do whatever she said.

It was an interesting note, Violet thought. Jobs trusted 2Face to watch over his brother. Not one of the adults.

The group, two groups, actually, were moving now. The bulk of Wakers carrying whatever branches they could rescue from the fire. A shifting mass of fireflies in the darkness.

Violet's group followed at a distance. She noticed that Jobs had retained the alien weapon. And they had their own burning brands that cast almost no meaningful light and indeed seemed only to deepen the impenetrable blackness.

They marched through the knee-high grass, fugitives again, running again. Leaving behind the shuttle, their only physical connection with the world, with their world.

Jobs and Mo'Steel were carrying Billy Weir by his hands and legs, like a sack of grain.

Violet wondered whether it had been a dream, an illusion. The sight of the boy floating in the air, rising above his doomed father, a black energy flowing from the boy to the man. Big Bill's sudden silence. Billy Weir's anguished cry.

"The nights could be twenty hours long," Jobs was saying. "We don't know when the sun will come up. Or if it will come up. Or if there is a sun."

The main group was pulling ahead. They were unencumbered by the need to carry anyone. They had more light.

"What are we doing?" Violet wondered. She was surprised to hear her own voice. She hadn't meant to speak.

"We're running away," Mo'Steel said cheerfully. "We are hightailing it. We are preboarding. Click on the X."

"No. I mean, what are we doing?" Violet repeated. "What are we going to do? In this place, this planet? Those Riders, the worms, someone taking the bodies, someone taking the eight people who might have been alive. All we do is react."

"Your mother seems to have a plan," Olga muttered.

Violet doubted that but didn't say anything. She doubted anyone had a real idea of what they were doing. And her entire hand hurt. And she was in no mood to just run and be terrified and be shoved this way and that.

"We need to figure it out," Jobs said.

It took Violet a while to realize he was reacting, belatedly, to what she had said.

"Figure what out?"

"We're getting jerked around," Jobs said. "We fly for five-hundred years, end up here, and all that's happening is we're getting jerked around."

"You assume there's some consciousness behind all of this?" Olga said. "That may be a mistake. People look at nature and assume there is intentionality. They used to think the sun was carried through the sky by a god in a flying chariot. Order does not necessarily imply conscious design."

"Isn't that what you used to tell your students?" Mo'Steel teased his mother.

She laughed, a melancholy sound, but welcome in the darkness. "Straight out of my intro to biology class at Cal State Monterey." Then, in a more somber voice, "All a trillion miles away."

"You may be right, Ms. Gonzalez," Jobs said.

"But you don't think so?" When Jobs didn't answer, she said, "Me, neither."

"The eight disappeared," Jobs said without explanation. "Ten percent of the Eighty."

"A message?" Olga wondered.

"I need to rest," Jobs said. He and Mo'Steel knelt to gently deposit Billy Weir on the ground. Jobs shook his arms, trying to get the cramps out.

"It's a base-ten message," Mo'Steel said. "I mean, ten percent, right? If someone's picked ten percent as some magic number, why is that? Ten's only a magic number if you got ten fingers. Otherwise, why not six or two or twenty-nine?"

"I'm in base nine now," Violet snapped. Then, the absurdity of it struck her and she laughed.

"Maybe it's intentional. Maybe it's partly intentional, partly accidental, coincidence," Olga mused.

Violet said, "If you're all right, then someone wants us away from the shuttle. They took the bodies away because they figured out that we were tied to them. They took the eight, the ten percent, that was to say, 'Follow us.' Follow us away from the shuttle."

"And leave the other five Wakers behind?" Mo'Steel wondered.

Violet shrugged. "Maybe they didn't expect us to leave so soon. Maybe they didn't know we'd panic and run."

Jobs grunted and knelt down to pick up Billy Weir's feet again. "I guess we sent a lousy message, then: Push us and we run away."

Violet could see that the main group, marked only by the ever-smaller points of light from their torches, was pulling steadily away.

By daybreak, if day ever did break, they might be miles away.

Her finger hurt. Well, what was left of it.

CHAPTER EIGHTEEN

"WHO ARE YOU? WHAT DO YOU WANT WITH US?"

Billy Weir knew he was being carried. He felt as if he was flying. Skimming low like a jet coming in under the radar. Fast. Moving so fast, no time to even look, no time to really see. Just a blur of darkened colors.

He felt hands wrapped around his ankles, hands around his wrists, he felt the strain of his weight. From time to time he heard the buzz of talk, and when he tried very hard he could pick out a word here or there, no context, just words. And he couldn't even be sure of those.

The sky was different. He could see the sky. They were carrying him faceup and he could see the sky. Not a sky. No, not a real sky, that was obvious. He could see what were supposed to be stars, what was supposed to be a moon, but of course they were no such thing. And beyond the illusion? Could he force his mind through the illusion, see what was real?

He tried, but gave up quickly. He was tired. Weary. Draining the consciousness from his father had taken enormous energy. Big Bill was a forceful man, he had a great will, and that had made it harder. Billy doubted he could have done it if Big Bill had not been so weakened. And of course he never would have but for his father's agony.

The pain had been a blinding glow, a green light enveloping Big Bill. As the pain surged, the light shaded toward deep purple, shattered into a rainbow of lurid green and luxuriant purple and night black.

It was a strobe in Billy's brain, insistent, the rhythm irregular, but stronger and stronger, firing his own nerve endings.

Big Bill had taken him from the orphanage and given him a decent life. He and his wife had given Billy love. Billy owed his father an easy death. He knew how to do it, though it meant spending the energy he had been hoarding.

Do you want to die? he had asked his father silently.

But Big Bill never heard or understood the question. He, like everyone but Billy, was a spark, electric, so fast, too fast to hear his son's slow voice in his head.

So Billy reached into his brain and found the answer himself. It wasn't hard. He had long ago learned to fire the neurons of another brain. He had long ago come to understand the architecture of the creased gray matter, the billion billion switches within, the ghosts of memory and ideas.

"Yes," Big Bill's brain wanted to say. "Yes, let me die."

It was like sucking a milk shake through a straw. Big Bill fought for life though he longed for death. Life and mind were separate, and life fought to persist, no matter how much logic argued for surrender.

In the end, though, Big Bill was too weakened by pain, by loss, and by fear. Billy had been able to give him peace.

Billy could feel the fear around him. Some of it was fear *of* him. When he let himself go, when he released, he could open himself to the minds that hovered like bright fireflies, like candlelit jack-o'-lanterns floating in the night.

The words in their heads were too quick, but Billy could read the deeper meanings, he could sense the emotions, the basic truths. So much grief, so much fear, so much guilt.

So much they didn't understand.

But then, there was still so much Billy didn't understand, either.

Who are you? What do you want with us? Billy asked, and he reached out, searching for the answer, feeling in the dark for synapses, trying to illuminate the architecture of a mind unlike any he had yet encountered.

The mind was out there, but beyond Billy's reach.

And not that mind alone. There were others.

CHAPTER NINETEEN

"YOU DON'T LIKE THE WAY THINGS ARE, YOU CAN GO, TOO."

They kept moving through the night. 2Face kept Edward close to her. He was a decent-enough kid, and she felt Jobs had placed the burden for his well-being on her.

In any case, it compensated somewhat for her fall from authority.

She fretted as she saw the faint lights of Jobs's group falling farther and farther behind. Jobs at least was a potential friend, her only potential friend aside, of course, from her father. Now here she was under the thumb of Wylson Lefkowitz-Blake and Yago.

Daniel Burroway was more a pouter than a fighter, 2Face thought. He would make sniping remarks, but after one particularly vehement dispute, Wylson had dismissed him curtly with the remark that he was "an academic, a book-jockey. This is the real world, not a seminar."

Since then Burroway had done little but stew silently as they walked along through the darkened landscape.

Wylson had absorbed the shrink, T.R., into her coterie and Yago had begun to draw D-Caf to him: a toady for the toady-in-chief. 2Face imagined that D-Caf, shunned by everyone else, was glad for any acceptance.

Wylson had dictated the gathering of wood for new torches, the assembling of any sharp stick or edged rock for weapons. She had directed that the line of march stay beside the river. They were wise policies, 2Face couldn't argue with that.

But she did object to leaving Jobs's group behind. At a rest stop, as everyone drank deeply, she approached Wylson.

"Ms. Lefkowitz-Blake? It's been hours now. If Jobs and Ms. Gonzalez or any of them had been infected by the worms, surely they'd show signs by now. We'd be hearing yelling or screams or something."

"That's not necessarily true," Wylson answered. "Parasites can lie dormant." She turned away.

"Your own daughter is with them," 2Face pressed.

T.R. intervened. "What you're feeling is healthy. You want to unite everyone, and that's very under-standable. Besides, those are your friends, no?"

2Face suppressed a desire to tell the psychiatrist to take a jump. She'd had to talk to shrinks after she was burned. She had no respect for the profession. But this wasn't the time for antagonizing anyone. She said, "I don't think we have the right to just kick people out of the group."

"Is it about rights?" T.R. asked. He wore a pitying smile. "Perhaps it's more about an unresolved feeling of guilt? We call it survivor guilt. The feeling that one has sinned merely by the act of surviving when oth-ers have died."

"I'm talking to Ms. Lefkowitz-Blake," 2Face grated.

"No you're not," Yago said flatly. "You're talking to air."

D-Caf giggled, then stifled the sound with his hand, looked at Yago for approval, giggled again.

Yago pushed past D-Caf and came right up to 2Face. "And, by the way, I wouldn't push your luck, wax girl. You and the freak-show Madonna and Baby

Yikes would maybe fit in better with Jobs and the Monkey boy's crew, you know what I'm saying? They already have that . . . that whatever he is, that Billy the Weird. You don't like the way things are, you can go, too. You can hook up with Jobs's freak show."

2Face fought to keep from showing the fear she suddenly felt. The threat was clear. Unmistakable. There were two classes of people: the normal and the not. And she was in the latter group.

She faded back from the torches, back from the clique around Wylson. She looked for her father. He was slogging along, head down. He wouldn't understand. Would he?

2Face stopped and turned to search the darkness for Jobs's group: If she was going to be exiled, maybe it was better to go voluntarily. She didn't want to be driven out like a leper.

She saw faint light, maybe the torches of the other group. Maybe not. A mile of darkness separated them. A mile of worms, maybe, and the alien Riders.

Besides, Jobs had asked her to take care of Edward. Where was he, anyway? She had to do that. Had to live up to her responsibilities. She couldn't run away. Why should she?

She touched her face. The burn had been horribly painful. The recovery had taken forever. But she'd understood it as an atonement for her sin. And after a while she'd come to see the disfigurement as a useful device for confronting, shocking, disturbing people.

She had abandoned her birth name, Essence, and taken the name 2Face. She had chosen not to hide her face. She thought of herself as an anthropologist studying the strange, inconsistent, hypocritical reactions of the people she met. Here is ugliness, look at it. Let me see your reaction.

But that was back in the world. That was back in a world where physical ugliness was all-but-erased by cosmetic surgery and DNA manipulation. Her split face, ugly and beautiful, had been a statement. And, she had always known, it was temporary — once the healing was complete the surgeries would begin. Twenty-eight square inches of 2Face's own skin had already been grown in culture at the hospital, ready for transplantation.

That world was gone. This was a simpler world. A more primitive world. "Unique" was no longer a virtue. Here people were powerless, and being powerless, were afraid.

No. She was not going to be pushed out. She was Essence Hwang. She had a scar. But she was not a freak. Not like Tamara and the baby. *They* were freaks. If anyone was going to be exiled it would be them, not her.

2Face threaded her way through the tired, foot-sore, hungry survivors in search of her father. He at least would stand by her. That was one. And Edward. Two. Who else?

CHAPTER TWENTY

"THIS IS AN AWFUL LOT OF TROUBLE
FOR OUR ALIENS TO GO TO."

The sun rose, small, distant, and weak. A winter sun. No longer a Bonnard sun.

Jobs called a halt and laid Billy Weir down. He was getting mightily sick of carrying the boy. They had taken shifts, but there were only the three of them, Mo'Steel, his mother, and Jobs. Violet, with her hand still leaking blood, was in no condition to carry anything.

They stood on a rise, not a hill so much as a low plateau overlooking a long, shallow valley. The river had slowed and now meandered toward a green, unhealthy-looking bay dotted with wooden ships that might almost have been the *Nina, Pinta,* and *Santa Maria.*

There was a village directly ahead. Strange, un-gainly buildings, some little more than rough lean-tos, others patched plaster houses with steep, dormered roofs. Jobs saw a brick bridge, arched, with a square tower. The perspective seemed odd; the relative sizes of buildings were wrong.

Within the village, people, all in costume, or what seemed costume to a modern eye. Men wore tunics and feathered caps, some wore crimson tights and brocaded jackets. The women wore white linen head wraps and voluminous peasant dresses and aprons.

There were pigs running in the dirt street, gaunt dogs, and chickens.

The people were busily engaged in a series of odd activities. One man in a close-fitting felt cap was facedown on a wooden table, stretching his arms to the left and right. Another man wearing only one shoe appeared to be trying to crawl through a sort of transparent globe. A man was shearing a sheep while beside him a man tried to shear a pig. A man armed with a curved knife was slamming his head against a brick wall.

It was ritualized, unnatural, not for a moment to be confused with anything real. The people were identifiably human, but behaving more like automatons. A man waded into the river waving a large fan and with his mouth open as if he was shouting. But no sound came forth. Another was perched on a steep roof and shot a crossbow at what looked like a tumbling stack of pies.

This unsettling, strange tableau extended into the distance, melding into a less-detailed vision of a crowded city. But dominating it all, overwhelming all with its sheer size was a massive building. It was round, built like a wedding cake but one that might have been carved out of a single mountain of yellowed rock. It was seven layers of arches, each set back from the lower one, so that the whole thing might in time have risen to a point.

But the structure was imperfect, asymmetrical. The top few layers of this stone cake had been slashed and within the gash, a sort of tower-within-a-tower, more arches, more layers.

Jobs turned to Violet. She held her disfigured hand up at shoulder level, trying to help the blood to clot. She was an incongrous sight in her tattered feminine finery, stained with blood. Her hair, once piled high, hung down unevenly, a fallen soufflé. She was dirty, like all of them, in pain, hungry, scared. And yet, Jobs thought, she had a determined dignity that he admired. And the truth was, her knowledge of art was proving at least as useful as his own technological facility.

Violet stared at the scene, awed, rapt, eyes shining. "I know this," she said. "I've seen this!"

Mo'Steel was salivating. "I see piggies down there. Where there are piggies there is bacon. And chickens. That means eggs. I am seeing bacon and eggs. I am seeing about a dozen eggs and maybe a pound of bacon, all hot, all hot from the pan."

Jobs was hungry, too. But to him the tableau was just creepy, impossible, absurd. Unnatural. "Talk to us, Miss Blake," Jobs said.

"I'm trying to remember," she said. She frowned and shook her head. "I forget what it's called. The style, I mean."

"I don't care," Mo'Steel said. "Question is: Are we going to get us some bacon and eggs?"

"It's like a video loop," Jobs said. "Each of those people keeps doing the same thing over again."

Miss Blake nodded. "It's an allegory, or a series of allegories. It's the kind of thing that would have meant more to a person of that era. Each of those people is demonstrating a fable or a saying of some sort. I don't recall the specifics. And of course there's the Tower of Babel, that's obvious."

Jobs blinked. He was exceedingly tired and maybe stupid. "The what?"

"The Tower of Babel. You know, Old Testament? Man builds a tower to reach up to heaven?"

"Jobs is a heathen," Mo'Steel explained. "If it isn't from either a technical manual or a poetry book, my boy here don't know it."

Olga Gonzalez said, "They're cooking fish. See? Not in the tower, down in the village."

"The Tower of Babel?" Jobs repeated.

"There has to be food, that's the point," Mo'Steel said.

"Brueghel!" Violet Blake exclaimed suddenly.

"A bagel?"

"It's a Brueghel. Fifteen hundred something. Six-teenth century, anyway," Violet said. "Look at the detail."

"Can we eat the pigs and the fish?" Mo'Steel wondered.

"Where are the others? Where is the main group?" Olga wondered. "I wonder if . . . oh, look. There they are."

Jobs followed the direction of her gaze. Perhaps half a mile away, a small, vulnerable-looking knot of people in shabby modern dress stood gaping down at the same scene from a different angle. They were closer to the river, just at the edge of the village.

"This is an awful lot of trouble for our aliens to go to," Jobs said. "I mean, did they do this with the whole planet? This all extends out to the horizon." He glanced at Billy Weir. He had formed the suspicion, the hope maybe, that Billy Weir had some profound knowledge he simply couldn't share with them. Certainly he possessed some sort of incredible power.

Unless that had all been a dream. Jobs could no longer be sure. He was exhausted.

"You slept for five-hundred years and you're tired?" he muttered under his breath.

"I guess we had better see if we can find food down there," Olga said.

Jobs had opened his mouth to agree when it happened.

A beam of brilliant green light, no more than two inches in diameter, blazed from the village. It drew a line at an angle to the ground. It seemed to originate from the small, crenelated tower at the end of the bridge.

"Laser," Jobs said. He frowned.

The tower blew apart.

Bricks flew everywhere. The half-dozen peasants closest to the tower were thrown through the air, tumbling, landing in the river, on the roof of a house, smashing into walls.

"What was that?" Violet cried.

With a shocking concussion, far larger than the first, the village exploded upward.

It was like a bomb going off. Buildings were flattened. Livestock was tossed carelessly, twirling.

The concussion was a hot wind in their faces, an oven blast.

"Look out!" Olga cried.

Twenty feet behind where they stood, a second beam of green light shone straight up out of the ground.

The first laser had been followed by two explosions.

"Run!" Jobs yelled.

They bolted, racing away from the beam, racing the only direction open: downhill toward the village.

The first, smaller explosion caught them, ruffled their hair, and rang bells in their ears.

The second explosion hit Jobs like a mule's kick in the back.

He flew forward, landed on his face, rolled in the sparse grass, rolled down the slope.

Violet Blake landed almost on top of him.

Jobs wiped dirt from his eyes and blinked. He was deaf to everything but a roaring sound in his ears. His head throbbed. He felt a sharp pain in his back.

All at once a hurricane was blowing. Olga Gonzalez was just standing up and the wind picked her up like she was an empty paper cup. The wind rolled her across the ground, faster and faster toward the ruined village.

Jobs snatched at grass, at rocks, roots, anything, but the wind had him, too. He was sliding backward, clawing, unable to hold on.

The wind got beneath him, lifted him up. He somersaulted backward and for a moment was airborne, flying.

He bellowed and flailed and slammed hard into a ruined brick wall down in the village.

Couldn't breathe, air sucked out of his lungs, grabbing at the bricks but they were coming free, each one he grabbed, falling, slipping. Then, a solid purchase.

He hugged the half wall and dug his fingernails into the mortar. He could see right into the village from here, right into all that was left of it.

He stared in horror as the wind picked up pigs and sheep, wood and stone, men and women, and sucked them all down into a ragged hole in the ground.

It was a whirlwind. A tornado. Irresistible.

Where was Mo? Where were Violet and Olga and Billy?

He had caught a hallucinatory flash of Mo'Steel running at mad speed, running with the hurricane at his back, propelling him. Then, nothing.

Jobs felt his lungs gasping, drawing futilely on thin air. He could not fill his lungs. No air.

No air!

He crept up the wall, climbed on battered knees and bloody hands, gasping for breath, up till he could look down in the crater left by the explosion. Already he suspected, already his brain was putting it together.

The crater was a hole, fifty feet across, a ragged, gaping gash.

And in the hole, down through the hole in the ground, Jobs saw stars. Black space and the bright pinpoints of stars.

"Not a planet," Jobs whispered. "A ship!"

CHAPTER TWENTY-ONE

"THAT WAS ENOUGH OF A RUSH."

Mo'Steel saw his mother lifted by the wind and hurled with shocking force toward the hole.

He jumped up to grab her but the wind hit him like a train. He did a Road Runner, milling his legs as fast as he could, but it was the wind that was in charge. His feet barely touched the ground, sufficed only to keep him more or less upright.

It was, a corner of his mind thought, a very woolly ride.

He flew-ran down the hill, into the village, un-stoppable, unable to offer any resistance.

He flashed on Jobs, saw a blur that might have been Violet Blake, blew past, wind rushing in his ears. If he hit anything at this speed he'd crush the last of his natural bones.

All at once the hole was there, right in front of him, right below him, down he went, down into a field of black, dotted with stars. It was a whirlpool, a sink drain, a vacuum hose, sucking him out into space.

Space?

Down and through and all at once Mo'Steel was sucking on nothingness. His skin was freezing cold. He knew he'd be dead in a matter of minutes, if not seconds.

He tumbled, weightless, twisted, saw forty, fifty strange, hovering creatures, liquid blue-steel, floating in space below the hole.

He turned, unable to control anything, nothing to touch, twirled, and into his field of vision rose an object so massive, so vast it seemed as big as a planet. It was a maze of protrusions, towers, bubbles, clefts, doughnuts, cubes, and pyramids.

It extended far beyond his field of vision in every direction. And it was beautiful.

Some surfaces were blazing bright as though filled with the light of a sun shining through green or red or yellow glass. Other parts were mirrored, showing nothing but distorted, twisted reflections of the stars. There were transparencies, opacities, glowing milky translucences. There were long streams of living light that bounced and curved and danced. There were shadows so deep they seemed to swallow light.

It was impossible to take in. He was an ant clinging to the undercarriage of a car, too tiny and insignificant even to be able to imagine the size and shape and purpose of the vast object above him.

Mo'Steel wondered if he was already dead. Wondered if his mind was already gone.

Then pain reminded him that he still lived. His frostbitten flesh slammed into something hard and unyielding.

He grabbed, reflex taking over. He grabbed and his hands slipped, numb, insensate fingers clawed at a surface that allowed no purchase. But he could wrap his arms around it. He wrapped his arms and held on, with his head swimming, lungs starving, draining the last molecules of oxygen into his heart.

He held on to the creature, the smooth, glossy, liquid-metal creature, as it fired engines within its hind legs and zoomed up toward the ragged hole in the bottom of the ship.

Mo'Steel saw the others, a cluster, rising all together with what seemed grim determination, up through the hole into the village, up through the hole in the hill. Farther down the ship, a quarter mile away, a second band of the creatures. More beyond that. At least four, five separate assaults, all taking place at once.

Mo'Steel held on with the last of his strength. Up

and up, up through the hole. Up toward a pale-blue, Brueghel sky.

Then they were through and Mo'Steel could feel the warmth, not warm but warmer than empty space. But still no air. Still his lungs seized and his diaphragm convulsed.

As if it had belatedly discovered his presence, the creature shook him off. Mo'Steel was ten, fifteen feet above "ground level" when he lost his grip.

He fell. He had weight again. He fell back toward space. Back to the hole. Back down/up into the stars.

He reached feebly, woozy, half-blind, trying to grab the lip of the hole. But there was no way, too far, emptiness beneath him.

And all at once a square of steel appeared.

Mo'Steel landed hard. His knees crumpled. He fell facedown, slid, jerked the wrong way, confused, and now his legs were dangling out into empty space.

Squares. Appearing all around. Ten-by-ten-foot squares, running around the hole, racing in a circle, filling in the gap, appearing out of nowhere, simply appearing. Like dominoes, they rippled. Coming toward him!

He yanked his legs up and a second later rested them on a solid surface.

Steel? Hard, anyway. The hole was closing, healing itself.

He was thinking. Yes. Breathing! Air, thin, but there. Thin better than nothing, a lot better. He had to expand his lungs to the max with every intake, gasping like a fish on land, but awareness was returning, oxygen was in his blood once more.

With an audible snap the hole was closed.

And now a wall of dirt was appearing, materializing. Mo'Steel was lying in a hole, facedown on steel, and the soil beneath the village was being replaced. It was like a wave rushing toward him, a ten-foot tsunami of dirt.

He got to his feet, ran straight toward the advancing wall, scrambled up, riding the wave of dirt like a surfer. He rose on the swell, windmilling his arms, kicking frantically with his feet.

And then, it was over. He was on his knees behind a rough-hewn stable. Two peasant women were doing something with a large copper pot.

He was gasping, sick, stomach convulsing, retching dry heaves, and still so cold his body was shaking like he had malaria. There was blood draining from his ears, blood seeping from his nose and eyes.

"Okay," Mo'Steel said, "that was enough of a rush. Even for me."

CHAPTER TWENTY-TWO

"WELL, SOMEWHERE THERE'S A BRIDGE."

Jobs watched as the blue-black creatures rose up through the hole in the village. Up through the hole in the hill above.

Machines or creatures or something in between, it was impossible to tell. They were quadrupeds, four sturdy legs supporting a high-arched body. They reminded him of Halloween cats, backs high. A head was carried forward, like any grazing animal might, but from the sides of the head grew two tentacles. They waved like snakes, like guardians of the face.

They were armored, metallic, blued steel that moved like plastic. Or perhaps the seeming armor was actually the creature.

The rear legs fired short bursts, like maneuvering rockets. They flew but not fast, not like missiles or even like jets. They lumbered. Like helicopters perhaps. Clumsy.

Up through the two holes they came, dozens of them. And Jobs thought he saw more in the far distance, behind the Tower of Babel.

They rose above the landscape, a blurry nightmare to Jobs's oxygen-deprived brain.

Then, air. A little at first, more. His lungs drew greedily. His head began to clear.

The hole was being filled. Squares of steel were appearing, plate against plate, rimming the hole, healing the scar, shutting out space. The steel plates simply materialized, entire, one after another. Like something out of a cartoon.

Now dirt appeared, eight or ten feet of it, covering the plates. Upon the dirt, right behind its advance edge, the buildings of the Brueghel village were once again taking shape.

The hole was healing. But the quadruped aliens had made it through.

They assembled in the air. Jobs counted. Hard to be sure, but he thought there were thirty-six. Thirty or forty, anyway.

They reminded Jobs of his own people, of the Wakers. They seemed hesitant, hovering, unsure.

"Mo! Miss Blake!" Jobs yelled. The risk seemed

acceptable: The aliens were ignoring the peasants that reappeared to populate the village.

"Olga? I mean, Ms. Gonzalez?" Jobs called. No answer. Oh, god, had they all been pulled out into space? What about the others, the main group? What about Edward?

He yelled again. No answer. He got to his feet and scanned in every direction.

Then he spotted Mo'Steel rounding a stable and felt a flood of relief. His friend was walking though the reconstituted village, carrying half a dozen pies.

"Mo! Over here!"

Mo'Steel came at a run, pausing only to glance up repeatedly at the hovering armada of armored aliens.

"Is my mom with you?" Mo'Steel demanded.

"I don't know where she is, Mo. Or Miss Blake, either," Jobs said.

"This ain't a planet, Duck," Mo'Steel said.

"Yeah, I noticed."

"This is a ship. We're inside some whompin' big ship."

"Yeah. And those guys up there just boarded it forcibly." He looked closely at his friend.

He and Mo'Steel watched the aliens.

"I was outside, 'migo. Caught a ride back inside

with one of those Blue Meanies. You should see this ship, Jobs. God, I hope my mom's okay."

The more Jobs watched, the more he became convinced that the Blue Meanies were space suits of a sort, small, individualized spacecraft almost. It was in the way they moved: not with the ease of a biological creature or with the speed and assurance of a sophisticated robot. They were clumsy, uncertain. Creatures within machines.

The hole was completely repaired. The village was back. The wall Jobs was on rebuilt itself, like a video on rewind. Bricks appeared, piled one atop another. He jumped to the ground and winced at the pain in his back.

Mo'Steel yelled, "Mom! Mom! Can you hear me?"

There came an answer. "Over here. In the barn."

They found her with Violet Blake and Billy, all in the darkness of what might have been a barn but for the absence of animals, or even animal smells.

"Everyone okay?" Jobs asked.

"What about those creatures out there?" Olga asked, ignoring Jobs's query and hugging her son.

"I don't know," Jobs said. "They don't seem to care about us."

"This is not a planet," Violet Blake said. "I was looking at space out there. Stars. We're in space."

"Seems like," Jobs said. He was distracted. Of course it was a ship, not a planet. Why hadn't he figured it out before? That's why the shuttle showed no reentry scarring. That's why the solar sails hadn't burned away. They hadn't landed, they'd been picked up by a ship that could simply match velocity.

It was the scale that had thrown him off. It was impossible to conceive of a ship vast enough to contain a tenth of what they'd already seen.

"Hey, you can eat these," Mo'Steel announced. He held out a pie for Jobs.

"What's it taste like?"

"Like you care? You live on jerky and chips. Tastes like . . . I don't know, maybe some kind of meat."

Jobs hesitated, but there was no point resisting. He had to eat. He took a tentative bite. "Tastes like . . . I don't know. Like chicken?"

"That's original," Violet said. She took a pie for herself. "It does taste like chicken. Maybe it is."

Jobs edged back to the door and peeked outside. He expected to see the aliens still hovering. They were, but now they had formed up into a V. Like geese heading south.

"They look like they're getting ready to leave," Mo'Steel observed.

"Hard to tell. They aren't exactly human."

The "V" formation hovered and rotated slowly counterclockwise. Then, with sudden, shockingly smooth speed, they jerked back clockwise.

They fired their jets and the entire formation shot ahead.

The lead alien ran smack into a steel plate that appeared in the air before him. Jobs could hear the ringing of metal on metal. The alien crumpled and fell.

They were all moving now and as each advanced, a steel square appeared to block him. But now the clumsy moves were abandoned. The aliens shot forward and up and around, dodging, zooming, accelerating, and decelerating. Some dropped down to just above ground level and blew between buildings, smacking carelessly into peasants.

"It was a ruse!" Jobs said. "They were playing dead! Hiding their speed. They were hiding their capabilities, playing lame."

It was a dogfight, a melee. The plates materialized, floating steel walls. The Blue Meanies evaded them.

The plates caught many. Many crumpled and fell to the ground.

But others escaped.

As Jobs and the others watched, a dozen or

more of the blue-steel space suits burned jets and disappeared beyond the Tower of Babel.

"I wonder where they're going?" Olga mused.

"To the bridge," Jobs said.

"The what? What bridge?"

Jobs watched them disappear from sight. Their flight was no longer obstructed. The defenses of the ship had either been exhausted, or the ship had simply decided to let the Blue Meanies pass.

"This is a ship," Jobs said. "We didn't land, we were picked up. We were picked up, we were attacked, eight of us were kidnapped. We're separated from the others. Now this. Well, somewhere there's a bridge, or the equivalent." He nodded as if to himself, accepting his own analysis. "Someone or something flies this ship. Someone or something's got an agenda. Someone or something is in charge. That's where those Blue Meanies are going. And I'll tell you what else: It's where we better be going, too."

It was a long speech for Jobs and he felt a little embarrassed. He was going to ask if anyone else had a different opinion, but Mo'Steel slapped him on the back and grinned.

"Sounds good, Duck. To the bridge, so my boy here can figure it all out. Let's travel."

A TOWER OF TROUBLE

REMNANTS™

K.A. Applegate

Landing on what seems to be a bizarre planet, the *Mayflower* discovers a structure similar to the Tower of Babel. While Jobs's and Mo'Steel's group try to unlock the tower's secrets, another group from the *Mayflower* wants to turn it into a home base—a place safe from attacking aliens. Now, in a mysterious land of unknown, tensions are running high and the *Mayflower* crew may be its own worst enemy.

Remnants #3: Them

Coming in October!

Continue the exciting journey online at

www.scholastic.com/remnants

REMW9